BREADCRUMBS
A Dark Fairytale Retelling

Twisted Tales

Leya Layne

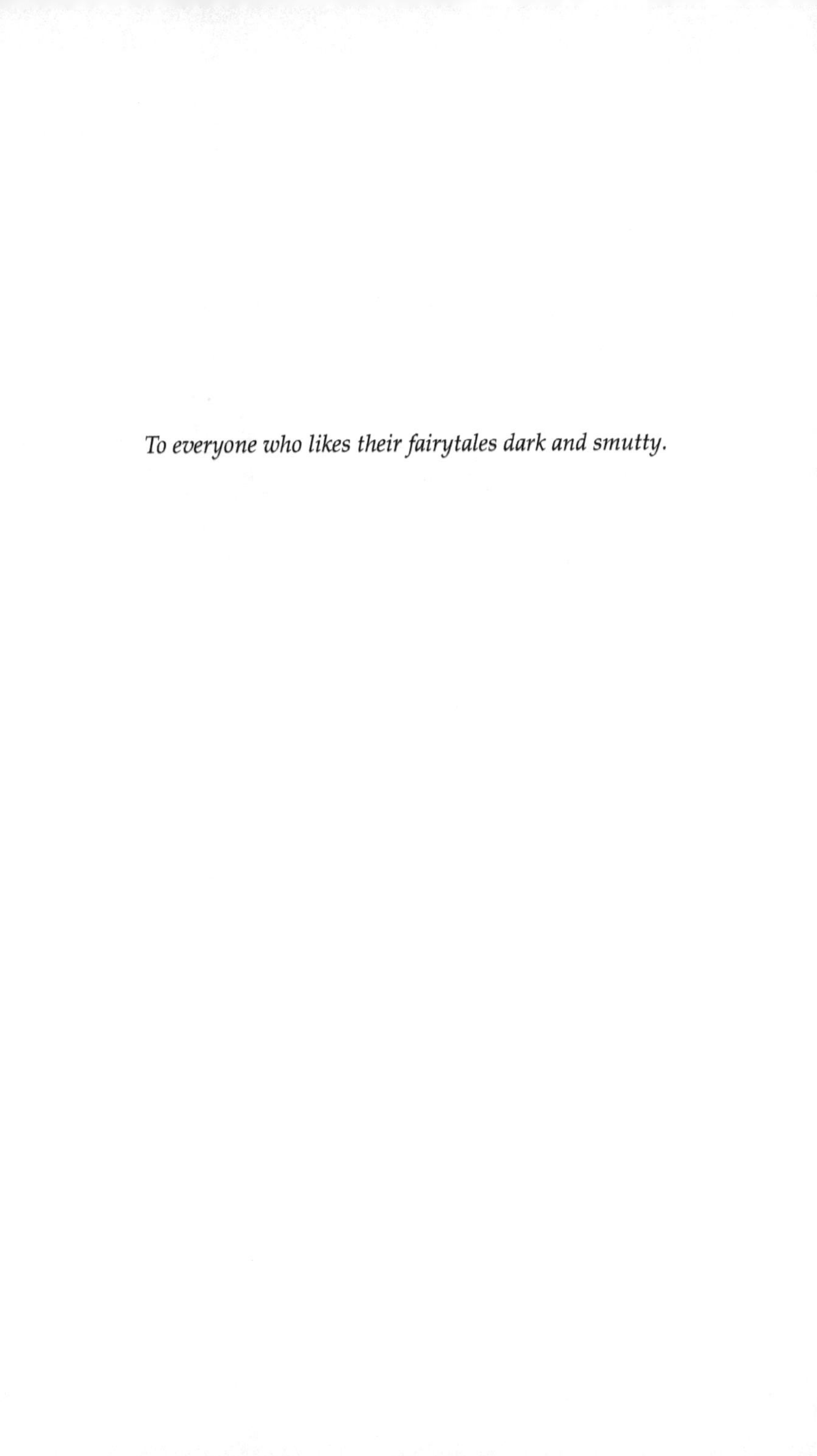

To everyone who likes their fairytales dark and smutty.

Trigger and Content Warnings

Usually, I simply add all trigger warnings to my website for those who need access to find and for those who don't to be pleasantly, or unpleasantly, surprised. This is by far the darkest glimpse into my mind I've allowed, and I do not want to chance someone being harmed by my words when my intention is to entertain, and maybe even titillate a bit. I have tried to include all possible triggers, but if I've missed any, and they're brought to my attention, I will update the list on my website. If you have concerns, check there first.

- *Taboo desires: Stepsiblings*
- *Group sexual encounters*
- *Involuntary drugging*
- *Sexual coercion*
- *Consensual nonconsent – Leaning nonconsent*
- *Somnophilia*
- *Choking*
- *Hostage situation*
- *Bondage: Locked in a cage and in stocks*
- *Involuntary anal with prep*

- Sex trafficking
- On-page killing
- References to childhood abuse
- Explicit language
- Explicit sexual content

ONE

Heath

Music blared from the top of the stairs, and Heath could hear Greta shuffling around up there. His mind conjured images of her dancing around in a towel, her hair a damp mess around her shoulders, and his cock stiffened at the thought. She was getting ready for a night out with some random guy she'd met online. She was always hooking up with someone. It wasn't that he hadn't also gotten his dick wet with random women regularly, but it was these moments when they were home alone, and she was prepping for someone else, that made him regret the agreement they'd made to be roommates until they each found the one. The one. Ha! How the fuck was he supposed to find the one when she was the only one he'd ever truly wanted? The one woman he couldn't ever have.

Thirty minutes later, she made her way down the stairs, and his breath caught. His eyes traveled up and down her body in the path his fingers itched to follow. She was absolute perfection. Soft and luscious, and unafraid to show her curves. She stopped at the bottom of the stairs, taken aback by the intensity of his stare.

"What's wrong? Is there a stain on my dress?"

His mouth was dry, so no sound came out the first time he opened it to speak. He slowly ran his tongue over his teeth and managed to say, "No, you look amazing." His voice was huskier than he'd planned, but she didn't seem to notice. Her smile lit the room.

"Thanks, Bro. You know my goal is to 'make their big dicks so hard,'" she said, mimicking a ridiculous movie they'd watched as teens.

She could recite damn near every word, and he couldn't stop himself from chuckling every time she dropped one of the more sexual lines. That reaction should be a clear tell that he didn't just look at her as a brother should because anyone else would have been groaning and cringing at their sister. *Stepsister*, he reminded himself, as if that made it any better. While he should've been groaning at her use of sexually charged lines and lack of clothing, here he was laughing like a fool with a raging hard-on.

"Who's the lucky fuck tonight?"

"No clue. Taking my chances at that new spot in the city, the one everyone's been raving about."

"The Candy Shack?" he asked, and she nodded.

His eyes narrowed. Though it bothered him that she was always hooking up with fuckboys from those dating apps, the idea of her not having a plan and going home with some random dude she couldn't even look up ahead of time pissed him off.

"Who are you going with?"

"Mel's busy tonight and Keilie's sick, so I'm prowling alone."

He popped up off the couch ready to tackle her to the floor if she tried to step foot out the door by herself. "Like hell you are!"

"Gee, dad, I didn't know I had to ask permission all of a sudden."

"Not permission," he said, his tone softer. "It's not safe to go alone, especially not looking for a hookup." *Especially not looking like that,* he wanted to say.

He knew he should stay across the room, but the compulsion to get closer was too strong. His feet carried him across the room faster than his brain could process his next move. His hands grabbed her shoulders, and he was staring down into her emerald eyes. They were wide and shining with complete trust, though he was gripping her shoulders in a way that could have been considered threatening. She trusted him, and none of the thoughts passing through his mind were trustworthy. He wanted to lock her away, tie her down, and show her just what some depraved fuck could do to her. He had deprived himself of her all these years and could feel how easily he'd lose control if given the opportunity to have her.

"Are you offering to be my wingman?" she asked, her voice steady.

The fact she seemed unaffected pissed him off. How could she not feel how much he needed her? How the fuck couldn't she see that he was dying, that this whole living situation had him tied in knots? And why didn't she want him back?

"Sure, let me get my cock-block gear on," he said as he headed up the stairs of their townhouse. Her laughter followed him, causing his dick to throb painfully. He'd always loved her laughter. When they were teens, they'd somehow often end up wrestling, and he'd tickle her just to make her laugh. The sound would always go straight to his dick. The feeling hadn't changed in the past ten years.

Less than ten minutes later, he was fully dressed in dark-washed jeans, a button down with the sleeves rolled to below his elbows, so his tattoos showed, and dress shoes. If he had to be subjected to her flirting with other guys, he could work on getting himself into someone as well.

"Look at you. Who're you trying to impress?"

"I'll let you know when I find her."

"Watch out now. I might have to steal her away."

"Wouldn't be the first time, you little shit."

"You don't mind sharing."

"Is it really sharing if I can't participate or watch?" He bumped his elbow against her shoulder.

"Hey, watch it. Don't bruise the merchandise!"

He gave her a sly shrug and held out his arm. She slipped her hand around to grab it.

Two

Greta turned in the arms of the guy she'd been dancing with, and he quickly started grinding on her ass. She pulled her hips away from him only to have him slam himself against her again. Quickly scanning the room, she found Heath watching her from the bar, and warmth spread down her belly. His stare was possessive and painful. How did he not know what it did to her when he looked at her that way? She lost all track of what she was doing and who else was around. At least she did until the guy behind her tried to squeeze the air from her lungs when he pulled close to ensure she felt his fully erect length. Her surprised look must've caught Heath's attention because his eyes narrowed as he took his first step toward them on the dance floor.

"You look like you could use a drink," Heath said as he approached her.

The guy she was dancing with tightened his hold on her. "We're dancing here," he said.

Geez. She should've known he wouldn't be the one when she hadn't even been bothered to ask his name. "Thanks, Bro," she said at the same time, keeping her voice upbeat and sweet to not show her eagerness to be away from the guy behind her. Thankfully, Heath stayed a couple feet back, so she had to step toward him to grab the glass he'd brought from the bar. How hadn't she noticed him carrying it before? Oh yeah, she'd been too focused on the look in his eyes.

"Get lost," the guy tried again. "Wait. Bro?" His voice was shocked expectancy.

"Yes, Bro. Now, let her go, and get lost." Heath's voice was low and menacing, a tone she'd not heard from him often, and it did things to her insides.

It had been years since she and Heath had gone out prowling together, mostly because his protectiveness could get a little out of control. Since the last incident where Heath barely escaped arrest because that guy had grabbed her arm hard enough to bruise her skin, they'd agreed to only prowl for women together. Tonight, however, that wasn't where her interests lay. She'd woken that morning from a dream about Heath and spent the better part of the day trying to contain her constant arousal around him. He'd just smelled so fucking good when she came downstairs to grab breakfast that she almost purred and rubbed against him like a cat. This whole roommate thing was getting harder and harder to maintain. Heath just seemed to get hotter with age. And now, here he was being one part protective and the rest possessive.

The guy's arm loosened its grip under Heath's glare, and she stepped free, grabbing the drink and downing it. She lifted onto her toes and kissed Heath's cheek in thanks. The guy huffed and stormed off.

"Now who am I going to dance with?" she whined, lifting her eyes to his.

"You're such a brat!" Though he said the words with a heavy sigh, there was mirth in his voice. She looked down to hide the smile that spread across her face.

He grabbed the glass from her hand and placed it on the

tray of a server making their way to the bar. With his other hand, he twirled her around, out and then back in until she landed in his arms with her hand flat against his chest. All the air left her lungs as he held her tight. She hadn't thought this through when she'd willed him to dance with her. His scent wrapped around her and traveled through her nostrils to her clit at a speed that should be illegal.

"What did you think you were doing rubbing your ass all over that dude?" Heath asked near her ear as they swayed together. "Did you think he wasn't going to pull you close against him?" He quickly twirled her back out away from him and then back in until her ass was pressed against him. "Or maybe you thought he'd ignore the wet spot growing on the front of his tailored khakis." He grabbed her hips with both hands until she could feel his erection. "If I can't control my dick with you up against it, what made you think some random dude would?"

She gasped at the intensity of his words breathed across her ear and the feel of his hard length pressing into her lower back. Fuck, she wanted nothing more than to slide her hands between their bodies and cup him. Before she gave herself over to the urge, her eyes caught sight of the guy Heath scared off staring at them. His look was a mixture of confusion and anger. There would be no more confusion if she started fondling Heath on the dance floor, and she didn't want to deal with any drama the guy might cause. With a sad sigh, she pulled out of Heath's arms, immediately regretting the loss of his warmth.

She turned toward Heath. Seeing the look on his face, his eyes blazing and nostrils flared, she quickly said, "I have to use the restroom. I'll be right back." Before he could say anything, she patted his chest with sisterly affection and walked away, all the while trying to calm the thumping of her heart.

Thankfully, the bathroom was empty when she entered, so

she was able to claim a stall quickly and chill for a moment. She took a few deep breaths, willing her overactive libido to relax. Her panties were already ruined, but she needed to be able to control herself from jumping on him when she left this safe haven.

A lone woman stood at the sinks when Greta opened the stall door and stepped out to look at herself in the mirror. The flush of arousal had died down, and her face was back to its natural hue. She looked over at the woman who seemed to be staring at her own reflection.

"Are you alright?" Greta asked, turning in the woman's direction.

The woman had gorgeous fire-red hair and a body to die for. Greta couldn't help but run her eyes over the curves accentuated in the green, body-con dress, but it was the woman's eyes that captivated her. Greta's own eyes were a shade of emerald that always got her compliments, but this woman's green eyes reflected light like the moss-covered hills of Ireland that were shown in every travel brochure she'd seen. They were bewitching.

"What? Oh, yes. I'm alright. I just got a little lost in thought for a moment."

Greta gave her a small smile and turned back toward the mirror fluffing up the curls in her hair.

"You looked like you were having a good time on the dance floor," the woman said, and Greta nearly jumped at how close she had gotten unnoticed.

"Oh," Greta said with an uncomfortable chuckle, "yeah, I love to dance."

"Well, you looked to be dancing less but enjoying yourself

more with that older guy. I mean, I'm sure he's not older, but he looks more mature than the first one who was banging his crotch against your ass like it was a bongo."

Heat began to creep up Greta's neck as she thought about how hot it was to have Heath up against her. Then she looked up into the woman's eyes again as the image cleared. "I'm sorry, were you watching me?"

The woman looked down at the floor before slowly bringing her eyes back up. "Maybe," she said with a breathy voice that made Greta's nipples pucker. The woman's eyes flicked downward, noticing the change, and Greta felt the heat of embarrassment quickly morph into a different type of heat.

"You put on a beautiful performance, definitely worthy of watching." This time, when the woman spoke, Greta caught a slight accent that she couldn't quite place. It somehow made the woman even more alluring. Fuck, between Heath and this woman, Greta was going to come without being touched.

"Thank you..." Greta paused, hoping the woman would fill in the space with her name. It didn't take long for her to oblige.

"Rosina," she supplied.

"That's a beautiful name for a gorgeous redhead."

They smiled at each other. "What is your name?" Rosina asked.

"Greta. It's very nice to meet you."

"Likewise, beautiful. What say we leave this noisy place and find somewhere quieter?"

She nodded her head in agreement before remembering that Heath was waiting for her outside the bathroom. "I can't just leave my brother," Greta said.

"Your brother?"

"Yes, the man I was dancing with last is...was my brother."

"You don't look anything alike. Wait, what does 'is was'

mean? Does one stop being a sibling at some point?" Rosina chuckled, and the beautiful sound sent tingles up Greta's spine.

"He's actually my stepbrother. Our parents married each other fifteen years ago, and we've been inseparable since."

"You looked inseparable," she said with a wink. "He can come with us if you'd like."

Once again, Greta's face heated. She'd come to the club looking for some dick to scratch her itch, but this conversation had her questioning that plan. Did she want to go with this woman? Absolutely. Did she want Heath to join them? That question was a little dicier. They had shared women before but never together or intentionally. The idea had her squeezing her thighs together. Rosina, seeming to pick up on her uncertainty, placed a hand on Greta's cheek and stared into her eyes.

"It's obvious you two want each other, but your reaction says you've never acted on that desire. You still don't have to. We'll just hang out and get to know each other. Nothing will happen you don't want to."

Greta took a deep breath and agreed to go ask Heath if he'd join them. She found him sitting back at the bar with a drink in his hand. Another drink sat waiting for her. She thanked him quietly, took a sip and quickly ordered a shot of tequila. He raised a brow, and she waved him off, turning her attention back to the bartender who handed her the small glass. Throwing it back, she let the warmth seep through her. Her entire body was on fire from all her illicit thoughts of the man seated before her and the woman who'd ignited something else entirely. Hope.

THREE

Heath

As they sat in the backseat of Rosina's car while the silent driver made his way through the city streets, Heath replayed the evening's events. He'd wiggled his way into serving as Greta's bodyguard while she tried to find some random guy to fuck, and she somehow managed to score a beautiful woman.

"I want you to meet someone," she'd said after returning from the bathroom. She'd grabbed his hand in one of hers and the rest of her drink with the other. When she went to step away from the bar, however, he pulled her back to stand between his legs. He couldn't help it. She'd run from his grasp earlier, and he wanted, no needed, to feel her close again. He had no desire to shake hands with some dude who'd get the pleasure of fucking her that night.

"What's going on, Gretel?" She rolled her eyes. She'd always hated when he'd called her that as a kid, saying that she could get lost in the forest even with a trail of breadcrumbs. Her response, however, shocked him a bit and made him follow her across the dance floor.

"Didn't you always promise to follow and protect me, Hansel?" She'd chuckled at her own joke, but when he didn't laugh, she followed up with another dig. "C'mon, ya big, bad wolf. I really do want you to meet someone." The ridiculous reference to another fairytale and her bright smile had him snort, but he finally got off the barstool and threw a couple bills on the bar.

Looking at the gorgeous woman sitting on Greta's other side in the car, he hadn't been prepared for the possibilities now running through his mind. The woman with her odd accent was absolutely stunning, and those electric eyes drew him under her spell. He still thought Greta was the most beautiful woman he'd ever seen, but there was something about this redheaded siren that unnerved him. The only problem was he couldn't decide if that feeling was good or bad.

The further they headed out of town, the more uncertain he became, and the more he wished he'd fought harder to drive his own car. There was no way he'd be able to find his way back through the maze of streets the driver took to get here, wherever here was. They'd turned onto a private drive with a locked gate at least a mile back, and nothing but trees greeted them on either side. *Where were they going?*

The heat from Greta's thigh pressed against his was the only reminder of her presence. She sat silently, seemingly unaffected by the directions they were following. Then again, the Gretel nickname wasn't just a play on her name. She really had no sense of direction and was liable to get herself lost going around a corner. He lay his hand on her thigh and squeezed. She finally turned to look at him, but rather than the normal brightness, uncertainty swirled in her eyes. Was she nervous? If so, what about? He was the one usually overthinking things.

"Welcome to my home," the woman, Rosina, said as the

car pulled to a stop in front of a two-story cottage that almost seemed misplaced this far back in the woods.

Rosina exited the car from one side while Heath climbed out the other and helped Greta behind him. They both stopped to look up at the light brown house with colorful adornments. The style was so quaint, Heath couldn't help thinking that the architect had gotten the idea from a storybook. There were windchimes hanging from each corner of the eaves, and flowerbeds hung from each window.

"This is so adorable," Greta said wide-eyed. "Have you ever seen such a cute house?" she asked him, and he could do little more than shake his head at her child-like wonder. It was only the skin-tight dress hugging her very womanly curves that reminded him she was definitely not a child. Still, he loved this side of her, the open and playful side.

"Yes, it's definitely not what I expected. The longer we drove through the forest, I thought we'd land at some haunted gothic manor, or some shit like that."

Rosina's laugh broke the spell of the house, and they turned their attention back to their host. "I'm so glad you find my home endearing and not scary. Please come in." She gestured through the open door for them to enter. "Would you care for a drink? There is a full bar in the sitting room. Help yourself." She walked off toward the back of the house away from them.

Heath grabbed Greta by the elbow and led her to the other room. He made his way behind the bar and found everything they could possibly want. Did this woman entertain regularly? There's no way she planned to drink this all on her own. As he leaned down to grab glasses from the lower shelves, he whispered in Greta's ear.

"Does none of this seem strange to you? This woman? This house? Its location as far off the beaten path as possible? The fact she has a fully stocked bar out here by herself?" She didn't respond, and he trained his eyes on hers. The concern had returned to them, and his heart sank. "What is it?" he asked, placing his hand on her cheek. She nuzzled into it.

"I'm not sure about any of it, but she offered for us to come hang out, and something about her turned me on, but I was already..." Her ramblings trailed off, and he found himself wishing she'd have finished the sentence.

"Talk to me, baby," he said before he could stop himself. "We can still get out of here if you want."

"Did you bring breadcrumbs?" Her laugh was sadly sarcastic.

"No, but I did bring a GPS. Thank goodness for technology, my dear Gretel." He kissed her cheek and continued making their drinks. She gave him a genuine smile, and his spirits lifted. "Here," he said, passing her a glass. "One LIT made just for you."

"And you mix drinks too," Rosina's softly accented voice rang through the room. "You don't know how to make a gingerbread martini, do you? I do like something sweet with a punch."

He pulled out his phone and opened the browser app to search for the recipe. His face dropped when he saw that there was no signal. "Do you have WIFI?" he asked. "I'll look up the recipe."

She shook her head. "Sadly, I just saw that it wasn't working. One of the perks of living out this far is the ability to disconnect from the world. On the other hand, being out here means I'm truly disconnected when my service goes down." She climbed on one of the barstools and faced them. Heath instinctively put his arm around Greta's waist, pulling her into his side protectively. Rosina smiled. "How about I just have what she's having?"

Greta stiffened at his side, and her hand came to his waist as if she were clinging to him for protection. Maybe it was just his imagination. He hadn't missed the double entendre in Rosina's question, but he chose to ignore it. No matter how much he wanted Greta, he needed to make sure she was safe more, and this sexy ass woman wouldn't deter him from that goal. Greta was his to protect.

"You two are cute. How long have you known each other now?"

"I told you our parents married about fifteen years ago."

"Yes, beautiful, I remember, but you didn't tell me how old either of you were. I didn't want to presume no matter how close you seem."

"Greta's twenty-eight, and I'm thirty one," Heath said while starting to mix Rosina's drink. Maybe if she drank enough, they'd have a chance of finding their way off the grounds and catching a ride home. He wasn't sure what the ultimate plan was, but he didn't think they should spend the night.

"Don't be shy, handsome. I like my drinks and my men strong."

"And your women," Greta asked from his side before making her way around the bar to climb onto one of the other stools.

She'd been so quiet that her question startled him, and he almost dropped the bottle he was holding. That was before the subtle meaning of her question hit him right between the legs. No, no, no, she would not flirt with this woman, not consider fucking her with him right there. They had boundaries. They had unspoken fucking boundaries. On the rare occasion they slept with the same people, it wasn't with the other present. He, of course, wouldn't say no to fucking this woman on any other day, but his reason for sharing Greta's lovers was always because it was the closest he'd allow himself to her intimate parts. It was a way to slake the unquenchable need for her.

As soon as the women found out he was her stepbrother, they always wanted to share the dirty details. For some reason, they thought to get some kind of emotional response out of him, but what they got was a physical one they could barely handle. Nearly every one had told him to seek therapy. One even went so far as to tell him to just fuck Greta already before he hurt someone else. None of them called him back afterward. He wondered how Rosina would handle his need. Leaning close to the bar, he simultaneously passed Rosina her drink and adjusted his hardened cock.

Rosina raised her glass, looked into his eyes, and said, "I like my women soft, delicious, and well-fucked," before clinking her glass to Greta's.

FOUR

Greta

Though Greta wasn't completely sure when it happened, Rosina turned on some music and invited Heath to dance. Greta watched the redhead slowly slide her hands up his chest and over his shoulders. She must've said something Greta couldn't hear because Heath broke out into a wide smile, and Greta wiggled uncomfortably in her seat. It was one thing when she was the one out there flirting with someone else. It was another thing completely to watch him with another woman. She didn't like it, and she liked it less because the woman he was dancing with also turned her on. Fuck, this was some strange hell she'd brought them to. When Rosina pulled his mouth down and nipped at his lip, Greta groaned audibly. This was literal torture. She slipped off the stool and walked over to them.

"Mind if I cut in?"

Rosina smiled seductively, and Heath shrugged, backing out of the way. Before he could move too far, Greta's eyes locked with Rosina, and the other woman bit her own bottom lip.

"I didn't say you had to leave," Greta said, hoping it would bring that smile back to Rosina's face.

When Heath stepped up behind the woman, essentially sandwiching her between them, Rosina moaned, and Greta's walls clenched at the sound. It was the perfect aphrodisiac. Her eyes locked with Heath's hooded ones, and she knew he was also affected by the woman's response. Would this be the time they truly shared a lover? The thought had her insides twisting in anticipation.

"Do you like dancing between us?" Heath asked against the woman's ear but loud enough for Greta to hear him.

"Yes. The combination of hard and soft is so delicious." The woman pushed her hips back against him while simultaneously pulling Greta closer to maintain their connection. "What about you, sweet Greta, do you like knowing I can feel all of him against me while I can also feel all of you? Or maybe it's the idea that if I wasn't the one sandwiched, you'd be feeling his hardness."

Greta's eyes opened wide, and she found Heath staring at her. She quickly looked away, heat crawling up her neck. Rosina grabbed her face in both hands, drawing Greta's attention when she mouthed 'it's okay,' before lifting her chin, so Greta once again looked into Heath's eyes. He was waiting for her response. She could read the anticipation in the tight lines of his face. "Yes," was all she said.

"Good girl," Rosina praised before pressing a kiss to Greta's cheek. The woman trailed kisses down to Greta's jawline and then nipped at the soft flesh right below the bone. Greta's eyes remained locked on Heath's. When Rosina pressed a kiss against her lips, Greta closed her eyes and gave into the sensation, kissing the woman back. Just as the kiss deepened, Rosina pulled away, leaving Greta panting. A tiny whine left her lips, and Rosina giggled. Then she turned her head and leaned up to kiss Heath who eagerly deepened the kiss. "Do you like the taste of her kiss on my lips, handsome?" He nodded without saying a word. She turned back to Greta. "Your turn."

Greta closed her eyes waiting for the feel of Rosina's lips while anticipating the image of kissing Heath like she'd wanted to for so long. She imagined his lips soft and warm, and pictured herself licking them before pulling the bottom one between her teeth. Lost in the vision, she moaned at the first touch to her lips, and a thick tongue probed deep in her mouth. Her eyelids flew open at the realization she wasn't kissing Rosina. The woman had slipped out from between them and stood watching with her lip tucked tightly between her teeth. When she caught Greta's gaze, Rosina smiled, all her teeth showing. Greta moaned again as she turned her attention back to Heath. She gripped his shirt, afraid to allow any distance between them. Afraid to wake and find this was just another one of her wet dreams. And she was definitely wet.

Hands grabbed Greta's hair tightly and pulled her mouth from Heath's. He protested with a loud groan, and Greta let out a whimper of her own. "My turn, greedy ones," Rosina said, turning Greta's head for another passionate kiss. She then repeated the action with Heath. The back and forth had Greta struggling to breathe, struggling to maintain control. She was on the verge of orgasming right there in the middle of the sitting room. She started kissing Rosina's neck and nipped at her earlobe. Rosina moaned around Heath's kiss. Greta's hand slid down until she cupped Rosina's perfectly round ass. She could hear the other woman's panting breath as Heath broke the kiss and followed Greta's lead along the other side of Rosina's neck. Rosina still gripped her hair, but instead of directing her movements, the woman just held Greta's lips against her skin.

FIVE

Heath couldn't believe what was happening. He also couldn't think straight with how painfully his dick strained against his jeans. Not only had he lost himself in kissing Greta, finally tasting her mouth, he was now engaging in shared foreplay with her. He slid one hand up and behind Rosina's neck, deftly unbuttoning the halter of her dress. The cloth slid down, exposing her naked breasts and peaked nipples. He ran his hand over one, cupping it and squeezing the nipple between his fingers before moving to the other. In a bold move, he continued running his hand from Rosina's bare breasts to Greta's covered ones. He desperately wanted to free her much larger breasts to see them up close, but he was afraid everything would stop if he crossed the line. Instead, he pulled his attention back to Rosina and took one of her nipples into his mouth, swirling his tongue around the tip. Her hand tightened in his hair and pressed him into her breast, causing his teeth to scrape across the nipple, and she moaned deeply. His cock twitched in response, and Greta gasped. He wondered how wet she was, and then his thoughts traveled to how sweet she'd taste. He had to reach down and readjust himself, though what he wanted to do was free himself and have her touch him.

"Yes, my sweets," Rosina gritted out between her teeth.

Rosina pulled Greta in for another crushing kiss, and Heath groaned with need. He was so fucking hard and quickly losing control. More than once, he'd almost reached out and slid his hand up underneath of Greta's dress while sucking on Rosina's nipples.

"Put my nipple in her mouth, Heath. Show her how you suckle them so well with your teeth."

Fuck! He could feel the wet spot form on the front of his jeans at her demand because what she said was not a request. She had no doubt he would do it, and he couldn't have said no if he wanted to, especially not after looking up into Greta's eyes. Her pupils were blown with arousal, and her mouth was already parted. He grabbed the back of Greta's neck and slid his hand up to fist her hair, guiding her mouth to Rosina's taut nipple.

"Stick out your tongue and curl it, like you would a straw." She followed his instructions without hesitation, and damn if he didn't wish it was his cock he was leading her to. "That's it, baby. Now put your teeth along the top of her nipple and slide them down, while your tongue wraps around the bottom." She did, and Rosina moaned, or maybe they all moaned. He couldn't really tell, but he reveled in the sexiest sight he'd ever seen.

"Uhhnn, you too," Rosina said, pulling his mouth to her other nipple. "Yes. Fuck, that's it. Roll my nipples between your teeth. Shit. That feels so fucking good."

With a sharp yank, she pulled both of them back up and then returned to kissing each of them in turn before pushing their faces together. Greta's mouth was warm, wet, and inviting. He tangled his tongue with hers and captured her moan in his mouth, mixing it with one of his own. They would never be the same after this night, and though the thought worried him, he was unable to stop himself. Instead, he kissed her harder, grabbing onto where Rosina had a grip on Greta's hair, holding them both close. His other hand slid under Rosina's dress and grabbed her ass tightly, his three long fingers sliding between her cheeks. He needed to do something with this pent-up desire, and Rosina would feel all of it if she forced him to continue kissing Greta.

"Can we take this upstairs?" Rosina asked as soon as his fingertips grazed her wet hole.

He opened his eyes and looked into Greta's with a hopeful question. *Please don't let me down, don't be lost to me now,* his eyes pled. She gave him one last kiss that damn near had him coming in his pants before pulling away to respond.

"Lead the way."

Six

Greta

Greta's voice sounded husky to her own ears, but she had never been so fucking horny. Their shared kisses had been better than any of her dreams, and all the feeling she had for him were running amok. The look he gave her let her know that she wasn't alone. They might not act on this all-encompassing desire, but it helped to know that he felt it too.

Before they took three steps up the stairs, Rosina stopped and walked back down past them. "I forgot I had put something in the oven. I don't want it to burn. The room is straight ahead, and the door is already open."

Heath's brows furrowed, but Greta pulled him forward. She wasn't ready for this night to end, even if all she was able to do was watch him with that beautiful woman. It would still be worth it. She grabbed his hand and led him the rest of the way up the stairs. They entered the room hand-in-hand, the tension growing between them as they took in the huge four poster bed.

"Nothing happens that you don't want to happen," he whispered, and she nodded.

"Make yourselves at home," Rosina said from behind them, and they both jumped, releasing each other's hand. She chuckled lightly, and the sound sent a shiver down Greta's spine. "I made some fresh toffee earlier today and put toffee cookies in to bake when we first arrived. I thought you might want to try them."

The treats smelled divine. Without hesitation, or maybe to distract herself from thinking about the three of them on that bed, Greta eagerly plucked a cookie off the plate and popped it into her mouth. She let out a moan of pleasure that caught Heath's attention, and when she offered him one from her own hand, he took it, catching her fingers between his lips. Her lip slid between her teeth. She wished she could feel his lips on the rest of her as the heat from his mouth sent shockwaves to her core.

"Poppet, you wear your arousal so beautifully," Rosina said, sliding up behind Greta and reaching around to cup her full breasts. She leaned back into the caress, allowing the woman to slide the top of her dress down, exposing the strapless bra that covered very little. Her dark pink areola showed above the fabric and lace. When Rosina removed Greta's bra and grazed her nails against her nipples, a needy moan left Greta's lips.

Though she'd wanted to close her eyes and lose herself to the feel of Rosina's hands kneading her breasts, Heath's movements caught Greta's attention. He had stepped back to lean against the wall, his hand pressing against the front of his jeans. Her gaze traveled up to his face, and she saw him licking his lips as he watched Rosina fondle her taught nipples. Greta moaned again, and he grabbed himself tighter, showing just how stiff he was.

"He looks delicious standing there fully turned on, doesn't he?" Rosina's seductive voice served to further her arousal. She nodded in agreement and wished she could taste him.

"Have another cookie and pretend it's him on your tongue." Greta reached out and grabbed one of the delicious confections, popping it on her tongue until the buttery goodness melted onto her tastebuds. The sweet candy stuck between her teeth, and she had to engage her tongue to clean them. She imagined running her tongue around the tip of the cock he was currently palming.

"So sweet," Greta moaned.

Rosina leaned Greta away from her for a second, but before Greta could lament the loss of body heat, the zipper of her dress opened, and the material dropped to the floor leaving her naked except for her pink lace panties that were completely soaked with her arousal.

"Your skin is so soft," Rosina cooed at her shoulder before kissing her neck and nipping at her earlobe. "So delicious."

Greta leaned her head back, giving Rosina full access to the delicate skin. She couldn't focus on Heath any longer. She was so near to coming, his desire might just push her over the edge. Rosina didn't allow her the reprieve, though. Instead, she rubbed her hand over Greta's sex and cupped it. "You're so wet, my dear. How soon before you explode from want?"

Greta's eyes flew open to look at Heath as embarrassment crept into her cheeks. His eyes were dark pits of desire, and his breaths were heavy. Her own breath caught when Rosina slid her panties to the side and quickly, without warning, slid two fingers inside her wetness. A whimper left her lips, and when Rosina pinched her nipple while working those fingers in and out, that whimper changed to soft moans.

"Your moans sound so good, beautiful. I can't wait to wring more from you as I drink your release."

At Rosina's words, Greta's walls tightened around the intruding fingers, and her breaths sped along with her heartbeat. She was so close to release, her knees wobbled, and her clit ached in anticipation. "Please," she begged.

"Please what, poppet?"

"I'm so close."

"And you will get what you need soon, my dear. But not yet."

"No!" Greta whined. "Don't stop!"

Rosina pulled her hand from Greta's wet pussy and quickly grabbed a cookie from the plate. Without a word, she offered the cookie to Heath on an open palm. He stepped close and swallowed hard before grabbing her outstretched hand. With the tip of his tongue, he licked his way from Rosina's fingertips to the cookie and pulled it into his mouth. Then he wrapped his lips around her fingers and sucked, moaning from deep in his chest. With every sound and movement of his mouth, Greta's core tensed. That he was enjoying the taste of her had her on the edge.

"Is she as delicious as we imagined, Pet?"

"Even better," he said, his voice breathy.

"Take your pants off. I'm going to taste her now, and you're going to fuck me while I do it."

He didn't hesitate, and Greta watched, her mouth opening as she took in his full nakedness. He was so beautifully hard everywhere. Her mouth watered to get a taste of him, especially once she noticed how the tip of his dick glistened from his own arousal. She started to take a step forward, but Rosina turned her away, leading her toward the bed.

"Climb up to the middle, Poppet, and let me worship your sweet cunt while your brother pounds into me wishing it were you. You'd like that, wouldn't you?"

"Yes," she said and nearly jumped on the bed.

The thrumming between her legs drove her faster. She

could hardly wait to have Rosina's tongue between her legs, and to have Heath watching her come was more than she could ever have hoped for. This night was going to be so much more than she had imagined.

When she'd flipped to her back, Rosina climbed between her legs, fully naked and immediately buried her face in Greta's pussy. Gasping, Greta grabbed her head and held it in place as Rosina's tongue flicked against her engorged clit. "Holy fuck!" Greta panted. "Shit, don't stop!" No sooner had the words left her mouth than Rosina lifted her head. Greta's hips followed of their own volition, desperate to renew the contact.

Rosina turned her attention to Heath who stood at the foot of the bed naked with his cock in his hand, stroking it as if in a trance. "You're torturing our little poppet. Put that cock to use and fuck me." When Rosina turned back to Greta, she gave her a wink and kissed her inner thigh. The touch was so close to her pussy that Greta whimpered.

The foot of the bed dipped as Heath climbed onto it and towered over Rosina's kneeling frame. The woman once again pressed her face between Greta's legs. Heath's eyes were dark with desire, and his cock stood out, bobbing as he took his position behind Rosina's tilted ass. Greta watched while he fisted himself, making long strokes before setting up to press into Rosina. Greta's pussy tightened in anticipation as if he were preparing to fuck her, and it was all she could do to stop from begging him to slide inside of her instead. Her head swam with images of him pounding into her from all angles, and she came in a blinding explosion as soon as Rosina's lips wrapped around her already throbbing clit.

"That's it, baby, come all over her face! I want to taste you on her lips."

His words sent another shockwave through her pussy, and she cried out again, clutching her fingers in Rosina's hair to hold her steady. The feeling was exquisite, so much better than any orgasm she'd ever had before. With her eyes closed, she took in the sounds of Rosina's labored breathing as Heath pumped in and out of her. Her imagination once again took on a mind of its own playing through images of Heath inside her, fucking her, not Rosina. She opened her eyes and found him staring as his hips rocked back and forth at a frantic pace that had Rosina filling the room with moans. Greta pulled her lip between her teeth, biting hard to keep from saying everything on her mind. She hated this woman between them. She wanted his skin pressed against her. She needed to be filled with him. Her nostrils flared in frustration, and Rosina laughed between moans.

"You're delectable when you're frustrated, Poppet. I can feel your desire and anger coursing through..."

Rosina's words cut off as Heath grabbed her by the hair and pulled her head up until her back bowed. He turned her to face him and attacked her mouth, licking and kissing. His tongue danced inside the woman's mouth, and he let out a deep growl that had Greta cupping her pussy. His need combined with the punishing pace with which he fucked Rosina's pussy had Greta ready to come again. Her fingers delved between her slick lips as she watched the two of them kiss. Rosina hadn't been wrong. Desire and anger were mixing together, driving her mad. There was something else too, something she couldn't figure out, but it was pushing her over the edge. Her lust was out of control.

Greta slid out from where she'd been laying in front of Rosina and turned around, settling her face under Rosina's upturned pussy. This position gave her a perfect view of Heath's length working in and out of Rosina. She could easily slide down a little further and pull his balls into her mouth, but she didn't. Instead, she slid her tongue between Rosina's open lips and licked her from clit to opening, allowing her nose to graze Heath's shaft as he slid out. The room seemed to fall silent around her as she took in his scent mingled with

Rosina's arousal. Returning her attention to Rosina's clit, she licked and sucked while rubbing her own clit, determined to come. Hopefully, a second release would relieve the impulse to pull his cock from Rosina's pussy and suck it until he came down her throat.

Seven

This entire night had to be a dream. No, something better than a dream. He'd dreamed of seeing Greta naked before. He'd dreamed of watching her come and hearing her moans echo through the room. His dick should've been calloused from the number of times he'd jerked off thinking about how sweet she would taste and how tightly her cunt would squeeze his cock. With his eyes closed, he pumped harder, picturing himself pumping in and out of Greta. Rosina, however, wouldn't let him live in the dream.

"Your sister's tongue feels so good on my clit. The two of you are so good together."

This bitch was going to make him blow with her words faster than her pussy alone would have. He reached his arm around and clasped her throat in his hand, stopping her from talking. At the same time, Greta's breath hit his balls making it hard to concentrate. She was so close to his dick, the closest she'd ever been. This night was going to break his resolve and every boundary they'd ever had.

"Shut your mouth before I finish first," he gritted against Rosina's ear.

"Harder," she squeaked out, her voice barely audible.

From over her shoulder, he could see Greta slide two fingers into her own pussy, making circles on her clit with the wetness. "Jesus Fucking Christ," escaped his lips before he could stop it, and his hips pumped faster. This would usually be the point where other lovers would struggle to handle him. Their talk of Greta's arousal and skills with her mouth would drive him into a frenzy. Then he'd choke them into silence and fuck them until they ached. Rosina continued meeting him thrust for thrust, taking every slam of his cock like she was made for it, and she still begged for more.

Their collective moans filled the room when Greta went still, drawing her knees up with the strength of her orgasm. He followed immediately and without warning, crying out. The pulsations of his release must have triggered Rosina's because she let out a whimper, her walls squeezing him. It was several moments before any of them moved. He slowly slid out of Rosina's pussy, and the tip of his cock landed on Greta's face. Rosina rolled out of the way just in time for him to see Greta wipe the evidence from her forehead and bring it to her mouth.

"Do we taste good, Poppet?" Rosina asked her.

With a look somewhere between sleepy, satisfied, and intoxicated, Greta nodded. Her legs were splayed open from where they'd fallen slack after she came down from her orgasm, and he watched her as his brain warred with the desire to bury his face in her pussy. Even after the strongest orgasm he'd ever had in his life, his lust for her would not be denied. He climbed off the bed and left in search of a bathroom.

He came back to find Rosina stroking Greta's hair as she slept. He leaned against the doorframe watching them. The moment was very intimate and one he wanted to join, though her hair was not what he wanted to stroke. He'd done everything he could in the bathroom to get the need for her out of his system, including splashing cold water on himself and jerking off to try and calm the raging hard-on that hadn't gone down at all.

"You look like a starving man," Rosina cooed, her voice soft and sultry.

"She went straight to sleep?"

"She's been dreaming since you left the room." He raised a brow. "She's said your name multiple times."

No sooner had the words left Rosina's lips than Greta called for him. It wasn't quite a call, more like a plea. Either way, his feet propelled him forward. This time, Greta's voice was more pronounced. "Yes, Heath, please." He looked up at Rosina who continued rubbing her hair.

"She wants you, you know."

His cock stiffened in a way he hadn't known was possible. He hadn't been sure of her feelings for him. He imagined the feelings were one-sided, and he was the one crossing the lines with how much he coveted her. To think she truly wanted him in the same way was more than he could physically handle. His entire body trembled with need as he stared down at her squirming on the bed, his name a chorus on her lips.

"You could have her. She wouldn't deny you."

Flaring his nostrils, he shook his head. "She's asleep."

"She's fucking you in her sleep. She's calling for you. She's wanting you. She's dripping her sweet nectar just for you."

"Heath, please," Greta cried out.

With a growl, Heath crawled onto the bed and slid his arms under Greta's outstretched legs, opening her pussy to him. She was absolute perfection, thick and juicy. He could see her arousal glistening along her slit, and his breaths grew heavy. His tongue thickened in his mouth, and he began to drool. He lowered his head and inhaled her sweet and musky aroma. Though his cock ached for her, twitching between his abdomen and the bed, he was going to taste her first.

"Her pussy is delicious. It's just like my cookies you've devoured, a delicate and sweet aphrodisiac. Take what she's offering you."

Heath looked up into Greta's face. Her mouth was open slightly, and her face was scrunched in frustration. "Make me come, please." Her words tore down the last barrier holding him back, and he buried his tongue between her lips, lapping her from entrance to clit before flicking his tongue in quick succession. He moaned at the taste of her. It was so much better than he had imagined during any of his wet dreams. His moans turned to growls as he devoured her, sucking on her clit and fucking her with his tongue. He couldn't get enough of her taste. He really was a starving man.

A feminine moan finally broke through his lust-crazed haze, and he looked up. Rosina had Greta's hand clasped to her pussy, using it to masturbate while continuing to stroke Greta's hair. Both women moaned at the same time, and Heath groaned.

"Have you drunk your fill, Pet? Have you slaked your thirst for her?"

"I want to fuck her. I need to fuck her, to feel her walls squeezing my cock."

"All in due time. First, I must lock you away for her safety."

He sat up, confused. Lock him away? He was Greta's protector. His mind flooded with thoughts of how he'd just devoured every inch of her pussy and the wild image he had of fucking her until she ached both for and from him.

"Don't worry, Pet. You will not be denied for long, but she must beg for what you want to give her."

He moved off the bed so fast, he surprised himself. Eyes downcast, he gave in to Rosina, though his body still ached to return to Greta. He missed the feel of her skin already, and his heart beat in echo to her earlier moans. Why then was he so ready to follow the other woman's suggestion? Hadn't she been the one who talked him into tasting Greta's sweet pussy? Wasn't she the one egging him on all night with promises of all his heart's desire? Now, she once again made promises with stipulations when Greta wasn't awake to agree or protest any of the decisions.

"You listen so well. The sweetness on your tongue has heightened your desires and made you more pliable. You are a beautiful pet, and you shall be rewarded if our little poppet plays along."

"What do you mean?" he asked, though his own voice sounded foreign. There was a hoarseness to it that wasn't usually there.

She didn't respond, simply led him from the room by his still hard dick. They went down the stairs to the back of the house past the kitchen.

"A long time ago, this room served as a larder, holding all manner of herbs and potions. Nowadays, I can have anything I need delivered, so I redesigned it into a playground."

The room she led him to looked nothing like the playgrounds he had grown up seeing. While there was a contraption that might've served as a swing and other apparatuses that could be climbed upon, he was sure more torture than entertainment took place in here.

"Don't be afraid, Heath. This will soon be one of your favorite places. But first, I need to ensure you won't break the spell before it's time, before our beautiful Greta is ready for all we want to show her. You do want to show her what you can do, don't you?" She gave his cock a few strokes, eliciting a groan from him.

It was then he noticed the cage in the far corner. It wasn't tall enough for him to stand inside, and it hung a couple feet off the ground. "You want to lock me in there? It's too small."

"Not if you get on your knees." No sooner had she spoken than she flipped a switch on the wall, and the cage settled down to the floor. "Now, get inside."

Again, he felt compelled to follow her instructions. What was it she had done to get him to comply so easily? How had she gained so much sway over him, forcing him to break his own rules and overstep all kinds of boundaries? None of his questions were answered, nor did he care because when she'd raised the cage again, his cock was at mouth level for her. She reached between the bars and pulled on his ass, forcing him to move tight against the bars as she took him into her mouth. His hips bucked of their own volition, and she laughed around his girth before releasing him and exiting across the room.

As soon as he was alone, guilt gnawed at him. His Greta was now at the mercy of that woman, and she was barely coherent. Was she, too, under a spell?

EIGHT

Greta woke with a start when cold hands slid down over her breasts and between her legs. She looked down at the same moment a warm tongue snaked between her pussy lips and found her clit. Her hips bucked off the bed, and her hands gripped the hair of the person offering her such pleasure. At the sound of the now familiar laugh, memories flooded through her. She'd fallen asleep after sucking Rosina's clit while they both came. The last thing she remembered was wiping Rosina's and Heath's combined release off her face and tasting it. The salty sweetness was a perfect blend, and she wanted more. But where was Heath?

She looked around the room, trying to focus beyond the exquisite feel of having her pussy eaten by a very talented lover. Finally, she pushed Rosina's face away, pulling her up for a kiss to ease the rejection. Greta had always loved the taste of her own arousal on another woman's lips, and she moaned while wrapping her legs around Rosina's waist, flipping them over. She kissed her way down Rosina's abdomen and slid two fingers into her sex feeling the sopping wetness. Rosina moaned, which simply drove Greta to add a third finger. As Rosina's climax drew closer, and she could feel the woman's walls tightening, Greta pulled her fingers out and stuck them in her own mouth, savoring the combined tastes. Rosina stared down at her and whimpered.

"Where's Heath?" Greta asked sweetly, holding back the concern that had begun to creep in when she realized he was no longer in the room.

"You were unconscious, passed out in post-orgasmic bliss, and he was eating your pussy. He didn't look like he was going to stop, he was so starved for you."

Greta squeezed her thighs together, though it was harder to do when she was already kneeling. She should be disgusted. She should be disheartened that he would do something like that while she was incapacitated. She should be anything but aroused. Yet, there she was, her pussy telling her what she'd missed.

"Where is he, Rosina?"

"He's downstairs. I had to put him away for a bit, so he could calm down. He was going to fuck you before you were awake enough to ask him for it. I knew you wouldn't want to miss that."

Greta narrowed her eyes at the woman. She may have been overly aroused, but she wasn't stupid. There was more to this story she wasn't hearing.

"That look on your face says I won't be getting your tongue again, huh?" Greta lifted a brow and slid off the end of the bed. Not bothering to put on any clothes, she made her way downstairs with Rosina behind her. "There's something you want to know before you see him," Rosina said in a sing-song voice.

Greta turned on the woman as soon as her feet hit the floor at the bottom of the stairs. "What's that? What have you done?"

"He's on his knees in a cage," she said with a shrug.

"A cage?" Greta's voice rose to a high-pitched squeal.

"He was acting like an animal, so I locked him away like one. His objective was clear. The only thing he wanted to do was fuck you. In my hope to protect you, I told him he'd be freed if you begged him for it."

"Begged him for it?"

"That man has wanted you for so long, and now that he's tasted your delicious cunt, he will not be satisfied until he has you. But you are free to say no as long as you'd like. He will simply remain in that cage where he cannot attack you."

With clenched fists, Greta stepped toward the woman. "Heath would never hurt me!"

"He nearly choked the breath out of me for want of you, and I'm sure I'm not the first woman he's taken on a rough ride while thinking about you."

Greta's hands trembled, and her lip quivered. He'd fucked some of her lovers before, but none of them had ever called either one of them back. Had he been rough with them? Had he fucked them while thinking of her? She'd dreamt of him so often while fucking other men, but she couldn't have imagined her sweet Heath, the one man she could always trust, to be a danger to her or anyone else.

"Where is he?" she asked again, her voice softer than before.

"He's in my playground waiting for us to come play with him."

Greta didn't like the sound of that, but she also didn't like the idea of him being locked in a cage like a wild animal. The reality of Heath's situation and Rosina's so-called 'playground' was beyond her imagination. It was a dungeon with shackles along the wall and boards with straps strategically placed along their lengths. There was a leather swing and a couch designed for perfect positioning. She'd had the pleasure of having sex on one of those before. There were also various cabinets that likely held toys and other equipment to mix pleasure with pain. Then she saw the cage. It was lifted off the ground by strong chains, and Heath was on his knees, his hands gripping the bars so tightly his fingers were white. His eyes were saucers with fully blown pupils, and he licked his lips when their eyes met. She took two steps toward him before Rosina's hand wrapped around her throat, holding her back.

"Not yet, Poppet. Though your arousal is strong, you are not ready for him."

"He shouldn't be in a cage. He'd never hurt me."

"Maybe he will or maybe he won't, but I said you'd beg for his cock before he'd get to leave that cage, and that is what I meant."

The hand clasped on her throat tighter, and Greta moaned at the same time she felt her air dwindling. Seconds later, Rosina released her grip and led Greta to a set of stocks that included a kneeler. She pushed Greta's head down into the cutout and linked her hands before closing the bar over her neck. The position of her knees, slightly spread apart and higher than the floor had Greta's back bowing, spreading her ass and pussy open.

"Does she not look beautiful like this, Pet, wide open for us."

The animalistic growl that came from the corner had Greta turning her head, eyes widening. There was no way that sound came from Heath, but there was nothing else there but him. He shook the cage, and she could see that his cock was completely hard, protruding from between the bars.

"Let me get her prepared for us," Rosina cooed. "She'll be begging for your cock in no time, and then we will fill her together. You will both get all of your desires fulfilled, and I will get to hear your screams."

Greta shook her head. This could not be happening. Her screams? Their screams? What was this woman on about? How had she manipulated them so much?

"Don't tighten up now, Poppet. Not when we're wanting to play with you." Rosina kneeled down near her face and pushed Greta's hair from her eyes. "Your screams will be from ecstasy. Don't worry." And then she disappeared from sight.

"Baby, are you alright?" Heath's voice came through, and he sounded more like himself. When she looked at him, though, he still had flared nostrils and the wide eyes of a feral animal when around a female in heat. "She's a witch," He said. "She has to be. That's the only thing that would explain the positions we're in and the fact that all I can think about is plowing into you over and over." Tears filled his eyes, but there was nothing sad in his expression. "Beg me to fuck you. Put us both out of our misery and beg for my cock. Look, it's hot and ready." He ran his hand over his shaft, stroking it.

Suddenly, cold hands spread her cheeks, and hot air blew across her exposed holes. "You're so wet right now, beautiful. You like the idea of begging him to fuck you, don't you."

Greta shook her head, but the gesture was a lie. She wanted him, and the way he was looking at her while stroking his hard length had her feral for him. She just wasn't ready to give in to Rosina's manipulations. This woman had already ruined any chance of her and Heath returning home to the way things were, the way they'd always been. How could they live together after this?

"You can lie to yourself, but it won't be long." Rosina's words entered Greta's psyche at the same time the woman's fingers rubbed what had to be lube between her two holes. Greta's pussy clenched at the feel, her mind wondering what

Rosina had planned. Then a finger slipped into her puckered ass, pressing beyond the tight sphincter. Greta gasped as a second finger joined in, stretching her open. "Look at that tight asshole stretching so easily to accommodate my fingers. Imagine how it will gap open to take one of my toys, or maybe it'll open wide for your brother's cock."

She addressed the next question to Heath who was kneeling up to his full height while grasping onto his cock. "Would you like to fuck her tight asshole?" He grunted out a response that must have been in agreement because Rosina chuckled and began working her fingers in and out faster.

"Do you think you can take three fingers, Poppet?" The only thing Greta could do was moan in response. Between the feel of Rosina's fingers fucking her ass and the sound of Heath's self-pleasure, she was on the edge already. She wished her hands were free, so she could work her clit and relieve the tension building inside. "I have no doubt you can, and will, take far more than three, but we will start there. Now relax."

Greta hadn't realized she'd tensed up until Rosina's words. She took a few deep breaths and let herself relax into the intrusion as that third finger stretched her far beyond anything she'd taken before.

"So full," Greta said between panting breaths.

"No, Poppet, this is just a teaser."

Then the fingers were gone, and a cold object pressed against her hole. It was slick with what was likely more lube. This time, the stretch came with a bit of a burn as it tapered larger, prying her open until it seated itself fully. Rosina had just inserted a butt plug in her ass. She'd never felt one before, but she'd seen them and couldn't imagine anything else staying in place like this thing was. It had her so deliciously aroused.

"Tell me it feels good," Heath said between gritted teeth. His arousal was a palpable entity in the room. The way he was snarling and whining, Greta was beginning to wonder if maybe he was a danger. Still, she was so fucking turned on by the whole situation.

"It's so good and has me so full. My pussy aches to be filled."

"Mmmmm let me do that for you. Let me give you what you need." His gaze darkened, and her pussy clenched again.

Without warning, a sharp slap sounded through the room followed by a sudden sting along her ass cheek. She cried out at the unexpected sensations. "Fuck! What was that..." Before she could finish the question, another slap resounded off her other ass cheek, and tears sprung to her eyes. She whimpered at the same time her clit thrummed. Just then, two hands grabbed her ass cheeks where they stung and massaged them both causing the plug to move inside of her, making her whimper in pain, frustration, and white-hot desire. "Oh my god," she panted out.

The massage was followed by another stinging crack of whatever Rosina had used on her, a whip maybe or a crop. She couldn't tell. "Fuck!" The sting came again, and she squeezed her eyes shut. By the time the hands returned to her tortured skin, Greta's entire body was quaking, and she was working her hips back and forth trying to find some kind of friction for her neglected clit, but her knees were too far apart. All she was doing was squeezing the butt plug on each forward thrust, making her pussy contract with a desire to be filled, to be pounded into submission.

"Are you ready for his cock yet, Poppet? Is your greedy cunt dying to be filled?" Something slid across Greta's clit, and she whimpered, bucking her hips involuntarily. Then it was gone.

"Please," she whined.

"Please what?"

"I need to come."

"That's not good enough. What do you need?"

The same thing slid against her clit again. It was flat and smooth, maybe the size of her earbud case. As suddenly as the sensation appeared, it was gone, causing Greta to cry out in frustration. "Fuck me! Rub my clit! Something!" This time when the item slid across her clit, it lifted and then slapped against the engorged nub with a sting just hard enough to take her breath away, and she nearly came. "Holy fuck!"

"You're a naughty poppet, enjoying your punishment. You know what to do to end this. Beg for Heath to fuck you. Ask for his cock. That is the one you really want. Don't be afraid to take what you need."

Greta shook her head. She was afraid of what this last step would do to their relationship. They'd already stepped so far over the line they'd been toeing for years, but she didn't want to ruin what they had. She wouldn't be the one.

"I bet your pussy is soaking wet right now and would feel so good squeezing my cock."

"I...I can't." She looked at him. "I'm..."

"I need you," he said. "We've scattered these breadcrumbs for years. Let's finally go home, Gretel."

His words and another clap to her clit broke her resolve. "Oh my god, fuck! Yes, please. I need it. I need to be fucked. I need you, Heath. I want you."

Within seconds, she was free, and Rosina helped her stand. The plug moved making her squirm where she stood, and her knees nearly gave way. "Prove that you're ready to take that plunge, Poppet," Rosina said sweetly while leading Greta over to the cage. Heath stared down at her with a hunger that had her heart beating from her chest. "Take him in your mouth. He's been waiting and hard for so long, he won't last if you don't give him some relief."

Her mouth watered at the thought of sucking his cock. He growled out a mumbled plea, and she took his head into her mouth. With an even louder moan, he reached through the bars and grabbed fists full of her hair, holding her still as he plunged himself into her throat. Tears leaked from the corners of her eyes, but she reached around and grabbed his ass in her hands, pulling him in further. He worked his cock in and out of her mouth at a grueling pace. There was absolutely no tenderness in the way he fucked her face, none of the warmth she'd always dreamed about getting from him. Yet, she reveled in his ferocity, in his need to have her. She moaned around his cock, and he cried out his release, spurting warm cum straight down her throat. She held him deep, taking every drop until the pulsing of his cock stopped. Only then did she allow him to pull out of her mouth before she licked the tip of his still-hard cock clean, earning a moan from him and Rosina both.

Greta licked her lips. "Fuck, you taste so good. I need to feel you inside of me. Please. I want to come all over your cock."

Nine

He must've died and gone to Heaven as those beautiful words left Greta's lips. She wanted him. Hell, she'd just taken his cum straight down her throat no chaser and didn't once complain about how hard he'd pounded into her mouth. The feel of her lips around his shaft was better than he'd ever imagined, and now he'd get to feel her tight heat. Rosina lowered the cage and let him climb out. His legs were wobbly from his climax and having been on his knees all this time. He had no idea how long it had been, but it was long enough for him to have lost feeling, nearly crumbling to the floor. With one hand, he grabbed the cage for stability, and with the other, he grabbed Greta, pulling her in for a kiss. His need for her hadn't slackened with that orgasm. If anything, it had grown.

"Come, Pet, let her take the reins this first time. You will be able to ruin her after your legs gain their strength again."

Rosina and Greta helped him over to the strange couch where they had him recline in one of the divots that pushed his hips upward, putting his cock on full display. He was no

49

sooner situated, than Greta straddled him and Rosina held his cock to her entrance while squeezing him tight in her hand. "Fuck," he moaned out as Greta began settling herself on him. Her moan was the most beautiful sound he'd ever heard.

"Oh shit," she said, her abdomen convulsing. "It's too much, too full. Oh fuck, I'm..." Her eyes rolled back, and he felt her pussy clenching him in the steady rhythm of orgasm.

"That was magic even I couldn't have conjured," Rosina said at his side. He smiled, not taking his eyes off Greta's face as she came back down to Earth.

"That was fucking beautiful," he said, reverence in his voice. "You are so beautiful, Baby."

Greta didn't respond to his words. Instead, she lifted herself before settling back down on his cock, taking him in completely. She repeated the motions a dozen times slowly before starting to rock her hips back and forth in a steadier rhythm.

"That's it, Baby. Fuck me. Ride my cock."

She leaned down and kissed him, sliding her tongue into his mouth and twirling it around his. He moaned into her mouth, and she smiled against his lips.

"You feel so fucking good. I always knew you would," she crooned against his ear, like it was a little secret saved just for them.

He reveled in her words, in the feel of her, as he fought his body's impulse to buck up into her with his years of pent-up frustration. Greta sped up the pace, riding him like a champ. Then, Rosina came into view, looming over them both. She leaned over Greta's back, and though he couldn't see what Rosina was doing, he felt the moment's hesitation in Greta's movements before she returned to her steady stride atop him. The stride slowed, though, when Rosina pushed down on Greta's back until she lay upon his chest.

"Wrap your arms around her, Pet. Help her relax."

He obeyed, though he could feel Greta doing anything but

relaxing. He ran his hands over her back and tried to pull her head to his chest when she turned to look over her shoulder and yelled, "What are you doing? What more could you possibly want? You have us fucking. In one night, you've pushed us past every boundary we've maintained for years. Isn't that what you wanted?"

Rosina laughed, and the sound no longer held the appeal it had earlier. Even her voice was beginning to grate on him. He would not feel guilty for finally being inside Greta, though he was not grateful for it either. He was in a purgatorial space where his body was still beyond his control, but his mind was clearing at a painful pace.

"Oh, my sweet poppet, I had promised you a thorough filling, and I plan to ensure you have it. I am a woman of my word. It is a shame how much I've had to do to keep you two stubborn lovebirds from making me out to be a liar. Now, relax."

Greta let out a small whimper, tensing slightly before relaxing, and the tightness of her walls against his cock slackened some. Rosina must've pulled out the plug. Though he'd had anal sex before, he'd never used a butt plug on anyone, so he wasn't sure the effect removing it would have on her. He kissed Greta's hair and ran his fingers lightly up and down her spine where he held her. Her sudden intake of breath, however, had him tightening.

"Relax, my dear. You enjoyed the plug while it was in, and this is no bigger than its full girth. You can take it, and you will enjoy it."

Greta shook her head against his chest, and he opened his mouth to say something when Greta moaned rather than whined. Releasing his hold, he tilted her face up to look at him. Her cheeks were pink, and she wouldn't look at him directly. The tightness against his cock returned, and he had to bite his cheek to keep from moaning along with her.

"Are you alright?" he asked against her temple.

"Yes," she said on a breathy whisper before another moan fell from her lips.

"There you are. I knew you could do it. You take two cocks so well, almost like you were made for it." Rosina chuckled before muttering something under her breath he couldn't quite hear.

Then, the woman started to move, the dildo sliding against his cock as if there was nothing between them. The sensation had him rocking his hips, pushing in as Rosina pulled out. They were both panting by the time Greta's moans filled the room.

"You like being fucked by us, don't you?" When Greta didn't respond, Rosina reached down and pulled her up with a hand around her throat. She nipped at Greta's neck and looked into his eyes as she spoke. "Admit that you like having two cocks inside you at the same time. Tell our pet here how much you want to ride his cock forever."

His eyes narrowed as he tried to figure out what her end game was. There was no way she was going through all this just to bid them farewell in the morning to live their lives, whatever those lives would now look like.

"Tell him. You know it's true."

Greta's eyes filled with tears, and one fell onto his chest as Rosina pushed her back down to him and began pounding in and out of her ass. He kissed Greta's temple, and though he wanted to do nothing more than promise her everything would be fine, he wasn't sure. He especially couldn't make that promise when his balls were tightening from the friction rubbing against his cock in the most erotic way possible. Just when he couldn't hold himself still any longer, Greta looked up at him, her eyes full of need.

"Fuck me, Heath. Please, make me come. I'm so full, and you feel so good, so warm and deep. If everything is going to be ruined because of tonight, then make it worthwhile."

He groaned in frustration and began moving. His hips

pumped up and down sliding in and out of her against Rosina's dildo. Greta began moaning in earnest, cheering them on, and he grabbed her hips, holding her in place while he bucked up into her faster and harder than Rosina could move. Greta might be loving having the two of them fill her and fuck her at the same time, but he would be the one to take her over the edge.

"Come for me, Baby. Let me feel you squeeze me again. Take me with you."

His fingers squeezed her flesh tighter as he continued to push her over the edge, and when she cried out his name, he let loose with a feral growl.

"Yes, that's it. Look at you both coming together for me. Your moans are like a melody." Rosina's singsong voice was back, and he hated the sound. Even in his post-orgasmic bliss, he hated this woman. Though Rosina had given him his heart's greatest desire, he hated the witch and what she'd done.

When Rosina slipped the dildo from Greta, he helped her rise from his cock before standing to his full height. Finally sated, his cock had relaxed, and his head felt clear. Greta's face was a mask, sparking his anger, which he turned toward Rosina.

"What is your deal?"

She faced him, her expression unreadable. "I thought that was obvious. I wanted to watch the two of you fuck each other for the first time. I enjoyed seeing how long it would take to push you past all the barriers you'd put in place, how much coaxing it would take." She smirked, and his fists clenched.

"You fucked with our relationship for entertainment?" Greta cried incredulously.

"Oh please, you two were already so hot for each other in the bar, I knew it wouldn't take much." She looked wistful for a moment. "You, my dear poppet, surprised me with how long you held out. My cookies barely seemed to have an effect on you until you fell asleep. Heath here, on the other hand, would've succumbed to a single word from you without any help from me."

"You drugged us?" Greta's anger was palpable. Heath had already figured out that she'd done something to them. The fact that he could barely control himself around Greta when he'd always been able to fight the urge told him something wasn't right.

Rosina scoffed. "I gave you what you wanted. I put each of you on a platter for the other. You simply had to take a taste. My cookies helped feed your hunger."

Greta grabbed Heath's hand and pulled him toward the door. "Let's go home. We'll work through whatever we must after..." She gestured widely. "all this."

Heath started to follow her when Rosina's laugh sent a chill down his spine. They both froze in their tracks. His heart began to beat erratically as they waited for her to say the words that would destroy the modicum of hope he'd mustered at Greta's promise for them to work through the night's events. At his side, Greta began trembling. He initially thought she was afraid of Rosina, but then she spoke.

"What the fuck is your problem? Haven't you done enough? Haven't you had enough fun with us? What more could you fucking want?"

Rosina's smile grew at each question, as if feeding off Greta's anger. "I have an offer to make you."

"We don't want anything more to do with you," Greta raged, and Heath stood by her side with equal resolve, though he also feared they might not have much of a choice.

"You might want to listen to my offer first before you respond so rashly. Morning comes quickly and decisions must be made."

"What the fuck are you talking about? What decisions? We've made ours. We're leaving!"

"First, you'd have to be able to find your way home without my help to get off the property. Second, you might want to know what will happen if you do leave."

"You plan to give us an ultimatum," Heath said flatly, not moving from Greta's side.

The witch smiled up at him. Admiration and a hint of lust mingled in her gaze. Any hope he had of building some kind of life with Greta died with that look. There would be no happily ever after for them. Greta must've come to a similar conclusion because he could feel her deflate against him.

"Good. Now, let us chat like civilized lovers." Heath's eyes narrowed at her words. "Well, we have spent the entire evening being lovers, so we should end it that way as well. Cordially, I mean," she said while walking toward the door. Before she left the threshold, a robe manifested over her naked body.

TEN

Greta nearly collapsed to the floor when she saw the cloth appear out of nowhere. She really was a witch, and Greta had given them over to her to keep from acting on the unending desire for Heath. All she could do was shake her head back and forth repeatedly, trying to make the whole situation disappear. Heath had always said she'd be the one to get them lost somewhere, and that's exactly what she'd done. Her eyes welled, and she squeezed them shut. She refused to let that witch get the better of her. Whatever it was Rosina wanted, Greta would make sure Heath was safe. Now was not the time to break. She clenched and unclenched her fists a few times before looking up into his beautiful eyes.

"I'm sorry," she said. "Everything's gonna be alright. I'll make sure of it."

He shook his head like he wanted to argue, but her resolve was firmly in place. She didn't wait for his response before walking through the door. Once on the other side of the threshold, she found herself fully clothed and had to steady her breathing. Realizing they were dealing with a witch and having her powers used directly on them so blatantly were two different things. Heath took her hand, and they walked down the hall to the room where they'd had drinks many hours ago. There the witch sat with her legs crossed and a glass of what looked to be wine in her hand.

"Please, have a seat," she said, gesturing to the couch. Hands clutched, they sat with their bodies flush against one another. "Here are the two options I present."

"Will either of these benefit us, or just you?" Heath asked, and Greta could taste the venom in his tone because her own mouth was also full of it.

Though Greta found Rosina's smile grating, it was far better than the woman's cackling laugh that had once seemed beautiful. After everything, she would rather hear the woman choking than laughing. Greta gripped Heath's hand tighter, wishing it were around Rosina's throat.

"As I was saying," Rosina continued without directly responding to his question. "You can return home, back to your life as it was, except you will never again be able to touch each other. Never be able to taste one another. Never be able to fuck one another, though you will remember every touch and taste you've had tonight. You will spend the rest of your days pining for each other."

Heath started to speak, but Greta elbowed him. She imagined him thinking that option not much different from the way they'd been living all these years, but he'd be wrong. They may have been wanting each other, but that was nothing but dreams and imagination. Now, there would be memories. There would be a genuine ache. It would be complete physical, mental, and emotional torture.

"Your second option would be to stay here with me. You would be able to love one another completely."

"What would you get from this choice? What's your price, Witch?" Greta spat out the question as if having to consider Rosina's offer disgusted her, which it did.

"You're still so angry." Rosina's words were a simple statement. She knew and was enjoying Greta's anger, which pissed Greta off even more. Though she tried to rein it in, her nostrils flared, and her lips pulled in tight. "And you are correct. There is a price, though I do not think it too steep or unwarranted."

Greta's eyes bore into the witch. The longer Rosina minced words, the more Greta wanted to strangle her. She had never been a violent person, but this woman, this witch, was provoking her. "You have already ruined our lives. You have twisted our love, toyed with our desires, and put us in a position to have to consider your heartless offer, so just spit it out." Again, Rosina smiled, and Greta closed her eyes against the red-hued emotions that marred Rosina's features.

"Should you decide…and it is a choice…should you decide to stay with me, to live with me, you will both serve my sexual fantasies. I will have you how and when I want. In exchange for you being free to have each other without the taboo of it, you will be my lovers until I decide otherwise."

"Either way, we are saddled with a lifetime of misery," Greta said.

"Is my love that miserable, Poppet?"

"Stop calling me that! I am not your plaything!"

"Ah, but you were just a short while ago, and by the look on his face," Rosina gestured at Heath sitting next to Greta, "you will be again." She stood and headed for the hall. "I will leave you two to decide. Just know that your choice must be made by daybreak, else the outcome will be far worse than either of the options I gave you. Choose well." And with that, she left them alone.

Greta turned to Heath, and he looked down at the floor. She could feel the sad resignation coming from him. "You would choose to stay here and be her pet, as she called you earlier?"

"I would choose to stay here and have you. I don't think I

could survive the memories of tonight without being able to touch you should we return home. I barely held myself in check before I'd felt you, tasted you."

"Do you think anything she's said is the truth? She could be lying to us."

"She could be, and that daybreak thing could be a fairytale warning meant to manipulate us into behaving as she wants. But do we take that chance? It's not like the sex with her wasn't good."

Greta couldn't disagree with him about that last part, but she also couldn't untie the knot sitting in her stomach. Something told her they would come to regret saying yes to the ultimatum, but she had no other arguments to make. They had to decide, and the clock was ticking on their next move. They'd let her win this round, but Greta was determined to find a way to end the game completely.

ELEVEN

HEATH

Heath woke with his head in Greta's lap. She was running her fingers through his hair while humming random melodies. He looked up to find her staring off into space. She'd been doing that often the past week, as if she were trying to escape into her own mind. Either that, or she was nibbling on Rosina's sweet treats far more often than he'd noticed. He'd managed to limit his consumption, though cookies and candy were ever present. Rosina loved to watch him lose control whenever the drugs hit his system. It was as if she wanted him to hurt Greta, to push him over some precipice. The vacant expression Greta wore had him wondering if Rosina hadn't succeeded. He lifted his hand to her cheek, and she sucked in a breath, startled at his touch.

"Shhh baby, it's just me. We're alone."

Greta shook her head as if trying to clear her thoughts before looking down at him. There was a sadness in her eyes that ripped at his heart.

"What's wrong? Did something happen while I slept?"

She gave him a soft smile that barely lifted her cheeks. "No, nothing happened. We've been left alone for hours now."

He blew out a breath. He'd slept for hours, hours that he could've been working on a way to get them out of this predicament. "Is she home?"

Greta shook her head again. "I don't think so. I doubt she'd have let us be all this time if she were home."

That was the truth. Rosina had kept them in a constant state of arousal, fucking each other and her all day for the past few weeks. At least, it felt like weeks had passed. He wasn't really sure that he could trust the rising and setting of the sun in this funhouse she'd built out here in the middle of a forest. It could all be an illusion that she'd created to trick them into thinking everything was normal when there was absolutely nothing normal about the situation. They'd been kidnapped, drugged, forced into this fucked up threesome, and left without any energy to try and come to terms with it all.

"You're probably right. Are you hungry? We could try and find something to eat that isn't sweet."

Greta shook her head, and his heart grew heavier. She wouldn't last much longer in this place, at least her beautiful mind wouldn't. Not for the first time, he found himself second-guessing their decision to stay. Maybe the constant ache of being unable to touch each other again would have been preferable to being under the witch's thumb.

"Well, I'm hungry. Come downstairs with me?" He climbed off the bed and held out a hand for her. "Please."

She took a deep breath, and he worried she was going to decline, but she then put her hand in his. He gave her a genuine smile and leaned down to kiss her lips. When she tried to deepen the kiss, he pulled away but left his smile in place to soften the blow. He would gladly kiss her into oblivion, but he needed food, and she needed a clear head. They needed to find a way out of this. It had been weeks since they'd met Rosina at The Candy Shack. Fifteen years of being family, nearly ten years of fighting his feelings for her, and that one fateful night made all their reluctance wasted. Their relationship is nothing like either one of them had dreamed, nor could they do much to make it better while stuck here.

He felt the smile fading from his lips, as a robe manifested on his body when they'd left the room, and he fought to think of something else. "Hey," he said, looking over his shoulder as they descended the stair, "do you remember that year we went skiing?"

Greta chuckled behind him. "Do you mean the year you fell on the bunny hill and broke your leg?"

"Hush. I'm not talking about that part. I'm talking about how beautiful the mountain was covered in snow and how pretty you looked standing against the floor-to-ceiling windows inside the lodge with that white backdrop." He sighed. "I think that was the moment I fell in love with you." The last words came out as they hit the first-floor landing before he turned to enter the hall that led to the kitchen...and Rosina's playroom. He shook his head. No, he would not think of that. He both loved and hated that room, but he didn't want to think about it right now. He wanted to focus on his feelings for Greta. He wanted them both to remember the reason why they were there together. They were there for each other, not the witch.

Greta squeezed his hand and stopped walking. The slight tug had him stopping in his tracks. "That long ago?" she asked, her voice choked with emotion. He couldn't meet her gaze, so he nodded his head in silence. "Why didn't you say anything?"

"You were my little sister. At least, that's what I had been forced to remember. Poppa made sure I knew my role where you were concerned."

Heath started walking again and hoped she would follow

along. More than anything, he hoped she'd drop that line of questioning. Of course, she didn't.

"What does that mean?"

When he didn't answer her, she let go of his hand and sped past him to block the narrow hall. He could easily have moved her. Her plus-size frame was nothing he couldn't easily pick up and move, as he'd demonstrated numerous times the past few weeks, but he wouldn't manhandle Greta outside of the playroom or bedroom, whichever Rosina preferred on any given day, really any given hour. The witch was insatiable and demanding. She was also holding them hostage for loving each other, and he wouldn't take out his current frustrations or terrible memories on Greta.

Greta put her hand on his chest, breaking the train of thought that had taken over. "What do you mean about Poppa?"

He closed his eyes. He didn't want to tell her any of this. That was not the reason he shared his feelings.

"Heath, I've been dying inside since my twentieth birthday when you..."

His heart raced at the memory. He'd been sent to stay with his uncle for six months. Six months away from her, away from his home, all for doing what he thought he was supposed to as her protector. They'd let him come home for her birthday party. No sooner had his foot hit the threshold than his legs carried him up the stairs and through her bedroom door without knocking. She stood in front of her full-length mirror wearing nothing more than a strapless two-piece bathing suit. He'd not seen her show that much skin since they were both kids, and the sight of her had his dick hardening before he could gain control of himself. She started to turn around when she caught sight of him in the mirror, but he didn't want her to see the expanding bulge in his pants, so he took the few steps to stand behind her and wrapped her in his arms.

It was supposed to be a simple, brotherly hug after they hadn't seen each other for months. Then her scent surrounded him, and when she reached up to pull him in closer, which was the only way she could hug him back from that position, he couldn't stop himself. He kissed her shoulder. Not once. Not twice. It was like he couldn't stop kissing her skin. His lips traveled to where her shoulder and neck met and lingered there.

"You don't have to say it, Gretel. I overstepped that day."

"No." She put both her hands on his chest, and the heat from her palms warmed him all the way down to his cock. "You stepped into the space I'd been keeping open for you but didn't know how to tell you. I was afraid I was just being a silly girl who was jealous of all her friends who were free to talk about how hot you were." A smile tugged at his lips, and she swatted at his shoulder. "Don't smile at that. You knew they all had the hots for you."

"Maybe, but you were the one I wanted. You were the only one I could see."

She leaned in and laid her head on his chest. "You never told me why you were sent to Uncle Hektor's house that year."

"I'd still rather not tell you."

"Please. I need to know what got us here. Help me make sense of the missteps before I succumb to the feeling that we simply deserve this." She waved her hand around with a sneer as if the whole house disgusted her when he knew it was simply Rosina and the ultimatum she'd given them.

He took in a deep breath. "Can I get something to eat first?"

TWELVE

GRETA

Greta sat at the kitchen island and waited for Heath to make them each a sandwich from whatever he found in the fridge and cabinets. Though Rosina kept them fed, she appeared to produce meals out of thin air most days. Between the tainted toffee the witch insisted they eat before every session and the magically produced food, Greta rarely found herself interested in eating. Watching Heath physically make the simple sandwiches, though, had her stomach growling. He smiled up at her knowingly and set aside two extra slices of bread. When he finished and sat by her side, Greta turned to him expectantly.

"You're not going to let this go, are you?" he asked between bites.

She couldn't. She needed to know. So much between them might have been different all these years. Not to mention, they wouldn't have been out prowling that night had she known she could have him. At least, she wanted to believe that she would have made different choices and not dragged them into this situation so willingly. He was probably right

67

that the truth wouldn't make her feel better, but it didn't stop her from wanting to hear it anyway. Thankfully, he didn't force her to beg him for the story.

"I don't want you to think less of me for what I'm about to tell you." She started to shake her head, but he pressed on. "I told you that Poppa had instilled in me that I was your protector. We might not have been blood, but I was your big brother, and it was my job to protect you." He looked at her expectantly as if to say, 'do you know what I mean,' before casting his eyes downward. She had nodded for him to continue, but he sat quietly, taking in deep breaths like telling the story was physically painful. She placed her hand on his arm, and he looked up with tears in his eyes.

"Heath," she said on a whisper, but she didn't get anything more out before he continued, his words choked.

"If you were out somewhere and got hurt, I got my ass beat, even if I wasn't there...or maybe because I wasn't there." Her eyes went wide, but he didn't pause. "I didn't know how to reconcile my growing feelings for you, but I knew that in some way, you were mine. It all started to blur. The protector role. The beatings that included repetitive reminders that I was responsible for anything bad that happened to you unless I did something to make it better."

She put her hand on his shoulder. "You weren't..."

He cut her off. "The day you came home in tears because your boyfriend had cheated on you and broken your heart, I knew that I had to do something about it. There was no way Poppa was going to let me get away with not doing anything. Besides, I was already jealous of the asshole because he got to call you his when you were mine. Those two things spurred an anger I'd never felt before."

"What did you do, Heath?" She clasped her hands in her lap to keep from reaching out to him again. Memories started to trickle in about that time. Paul had broken her heart. They were nineteen, still kids, but she thought he was going to be her forever love. Then she caught him walking out of his parents' barn with Tracy, both of them with hay in their hair. He didn't even have the decency to look remorseful. When Tracy started laughing, Greta had walked away, not wanting to let them see her tears. She'd run home and into Heath's arms, pouring her pain out to him. He'd held her and brushed his hands over her hair. He'd promised that he'd make things better. Then he'd left the house, and she didn't see him again for months. It was like the hole she'd thought Paul put in her heart stretched to an impossible size with Heath's absence. She'd lost them both in the same day. "Poppa returned that night and said you went home with Uncle Hektor. I didn't even know he was in town."

"He wasn't. Poppa called him when I came back to the house."

"You came back?" That didn't make any sense. She'd waited up for him. She'd waited for days. Then the days turned to weeks and weeks to months.

"Well, I didn't actually make it to the house. Poppa found me walking toward home. The fact no one else had seen me, had seen what I looked like, was the only reason I was able to go to Uncle Hektor's."

Greta lifted his chin with her fingers, her eyes pleading for answers her brain knew she did not want. "What did you do, Heath?"

"I did what I was supposed to do to make it better. I made sure that asshole would never hurt you again."

She gasped at the implication of his words. She shook her head, trying to make sense of it all, trying to reconcile her protective brother with someone who could just make someone else disappear. She should be upset by his confession, but she wasn't. The pieces of her memories started to fall into place. "I was so upset about you leaving without telling me that I completely forgot about Paul's disappearance." Heath made a sound like a growl deep in his throat at the mention of Paul's name. She took a few steadying breaths. "Poppa sent you away to protect you?"

Heath laughed. "I think it more likely that he sent me away to protect you. He'd have let me rot or punished me himself had I not dealt with that asshole, but he wouldn't have let anyone drag you into the spotlight as the reason why I did it. You weren't his blood, but you were his favorite."

"Until I said I was moving in with you in the city." Tears burned her eyes, and she sniffed back the sob threatening to escape. Her stepfather was the one person she always thought she could depend on aside from Heath. Even after her mother's untimely death, he continued to dote on her, to protect her. When he'd decided to remarry again, Greta didn't want to remain at home between them. It was too hard to remember her mom while another woman was in the house. That was when Heath and she had decided to become roommates until they found their soulmates. At least, that's how the joke went. Poppa didn't see it as a joke, though. He saw it as a betrayal, that she was choosing Heath over him, which made no sense.

"I believe Poppa had guessed my feelings for you long before and decided I was no longer safe. He didn't even want me coming back around the house after your twentieth birthday party."

She moved closer and put her hand to his cheek. "He was wrong."

"I'm not so sure. He called me every name in the book and forbid me from spending time with you. He wouldn't even take my calls after that, his own son. I was shocked when he'd asked to see me after you told him you were moving in with me. I hadn't seen him in almost two years at that point."

"You've talked to him? He stopped talking to me almost immediately."

Heath took a deep breath and blew it out as if releasing the final vestiges of his resolve before speaking again. "The day I met with him, he was pissed. According to him, I had coerced you into moving into the city. He couldn't believe that you'd made the decision yourself or that you had been the one to suggest we become roommates."

"What? Why would he do that?"

"He was fucking delusional. He couldn't ever be wrong. In fact, he was so sure that I had somehow manipulated the situation that he chased me down in his car when I walked out of the bar where we'd met. Finally, I stopped alongside of the road, ready to tell him to fuck himself. Before I could get a word out, he swung at me. I barely stepped back out of reach." Greta couldn't believe what she was hearing, but she was too stunned to say anything. Fear gripped her chest as Heath laid it all out.

"He was screaming at me, telling me how disappointed in me he was and how selfish I was for trying to keep you to myself. 'I told you to protect her, not fuck her,' he'd yelled, and I lost it. Other than that time I kissed you on your birthday, I'd not touched you. I'd kept my distance. I'd done everything he told me to do, and still, I couldn't do anything right. For him to accuse me of fucking you when I'd spent all those years keeping my hands to myself...I couldn't take it. I punched him in his jaw, and once I made that first contact, I couldn't stop. So many years of being his punching bag. So many years of being talked down to. I couldn't see through the tears, but his face was bloody by the time I caught my breath."

Heath's head dropped and his shoulders shook when he stopped talking. Greta turned completely and put her arms around him, pulling him to her chest. She tried her best to console him, though her mind was reeling from the revelations. She'd learned so much about Heath since they'd been here with Rosina, and it was still hard to reconcile the man she'd known all these years with the person he'd kept hidden from her. She should be disgusted or afraid of him, but she wasn't. If there was anything she knew, it was that he would not hurt her. Everything he told her proved that even further. He'd protected her from everyone, including himself. He was her only safe place.

"Hey," she said softly, kissing the top of his head as she stood to be closer to him. His arms came around her waist, and she pressed her body closer. Leaning down, she kissed his temple and then his jaw. "I'm so sorry you had to deal with all that alone. I didn't know." She pulled on his knee until he turned enough that she could step between his legs. "You're not alone anymore, Heath. I'm here with you."

THIRTEEN

You're not alone anymore.

Greta's words rang through his head, ricocheting off every negative emotion and disparaging words of self-loathing that had stirred within his mind as he recounted his poor life choices. He'd killed people. Hell, he'd killed his own father. The anger he'd felt at those two men was so overwhelming that they were both laying on the ground at his feet before he even realized what was happening. He could hardly remember the acts, but he remembered the anger. They'd hurt her or put him in a position to hurt her. His whole world revolved around protecting Greta, and they'd acted like he wouldn't fulfill his promise as her big brother. Then he remembered that he hadn't treated her like a big brother would these past weeks. He'd stepped way over the line from protector to possessor.

She kissed him again, her mouth tracing from his jaw to his neck and back up to his earlobe, and he forgot about his promises. "Shhhh." The sound reverberated through his ear, down his spine, and into his cock. "Let me take care of you for once." Without warning, his length was pressing into the flesh of her midsection where she stood between his legs. She smiled up at him as her hand wrapped around his length. He slipped his hand around the back of her neck, pulling her in for a crushing kiss.

"You don't..."

Greta didn't let him finish. She squatted in front of him and took him into her mouth. The words died, and all that left his lips was a soft moan as her tongue slid down his length. He grabbed her hair, smoothing it back from her face, so he could watch her movements. Her cheeks hollowed out, and his eyes rolled back.

"Starting without me, are you?" Rosina's voice called from the hall.

They both froze, and Heath let out an inhuman snarl. He could not hate this woman more than he did in that moment. All he wanted was time alone with Greta, time for them to just be, and this bitch had to come home. It was almost like she knew exactly what they were doing at all times. Without removing his hands from Greta's hair or letting her pull from him, he gave a hurried glance over the entire kitchen. Did the witch have cameras set up around the house? Could she hear their conversations? If so, did she hear his confessions. A shudder ran through him and not from Greta's mouth on his cock.

When Rosina stepped into the kitchen dressed impeccably in a tailored pencil skirt and button-down blouse with six-inch heels, Greta started to stand.

"Don't stop, Poppet. Heath looked to be enjoying himself. I told you that you could have each other whenever you wanted while you were here. I'm a woman of my word."

Heath looked down into Greta's eyes that were lifted to his in question. She looked so fucking beautiful like that with nothing but love in her gaze and his cock in her mouth. He couldn't say no, though he still wished Rosina would go back to wherever the fuck she'd been all day. They deserved a moment of intimacy that was just theirs, but it was too much to ask for because the witch approached them from the doorway, lust shining in her eyes. She ran her hands over his shoulders, softly caressing his taut muscles before leaning down to whisper in his ear.

"You can't hide from me, Pet. I see what's in your heart, and I know that darkness lurks in you." She ran her tongue along his ear. "You're angry I'm here, but your anger is delicious. You fuck me so well when you're angry."

He closed his eyes. She knew. Somehow, she knew what he told Greta, and he knew she was going to use it against him.

FOURTEEN

If that bitch thought Heath was angry, she had to feel the disdain seeping from Greta's pores. She'd come to despise the woman who was not only holding them hostage for her own sexual gratification but also encroaching on their limited alone time. Rosina was right. She had promised they could enjoy each other at any time, but she never fucking left them alone to do it. Now, here she was walking in on them finding comfort with each other, and she had to interject herself. With every second Rosina hovered over them, Greta's anger grew until it was close to boiling over. Heath began running his fingers through her hair, both holding her in place on his cock and trying to calm her emotions. She knew he was only trying to keep her from saying something that might cause more trouble for them, but she was past caring. Then something happened that nearly made her bite down as her whole body tensed.

A man's voice reverberated from the hall. "Rosina, I got everything inside and put away."

"We're in the kitchen."

The amusement in Rosina's tone made Greta's blood run cold. Heath quickly pulled Greta from his cock, lifting her by the arms until she was standing between his legs. Rosina looked over her shoulder at them and smiled, a wicked gleam in her eye. Heath must've had a similar response to Greta's because he wrapped his arm around her waist and pulled her closer. If he had been standing, Greta had no doubt, he'd have pushed her behind him for protection.

"What do we have here?" the man asked, his gaze running over Greta's body, as if the robe had disappeared again, and landing on the arm firmly wrapped around her.

For the first time in her life, Greta wished she were smaller, small enough to be invisible. The man's eyes flicked between Greta and Heath, and a lecherous grin spread across his lips. Instinctively, Greta reached her hands around to hold Heath behind her, as if she could shield him from the man. Something about him looking at them both as a collective prize he'd won repulsed her.

"My guests had just finished their lunch and were getting ready to enjoy some dessert. It seems we made it just in time to join them."

Rosina's sickeningly sweet tone had bile burning Greta's throat even before the witch turned to introduce him. "This is my driver and friend, Otho. He runs all my errands and occasionally comes to enjoy a game or two."

The man-bear chuckled. "They don't look like they were expecting company."

"No matter. It's my house and my games. I make the rules."

This couldn't be happening. There was no way the witch intended to share them with this ogre of a man. Even if he hadn't been the size of a bear, taking up the entire doorway, the scars that crisscrossed his face would've been enough to repulse Greta. She had no doubt he could tear her in two with his bare hands if he chose to do so. She started shaking her head back and forth before she could stop herself, and his smile only grew.

Rosina reached up into the cabinet nearest the fridge and pulled down a cookie jar in the shape of a birdcage. Heath flinched, and Greta grabbed his hands where they were clamped around her. He'd only been locked in Rosina's cage once, but it had taken a toll on him. The number of times he'd apologized to Greta for leaving her unprotected against the witch was proof. The way he trembled now, whether in fear or rage, was further testament to how those hours had affected him.

"Shhhh," Greta cooed quietly while stroking his hands and wrists.

"Let's have some milk and cookies while you get to know Otho. You'll find he's not as much of a brute as he looks. I've known him to be quite gentle at times."

"I can be gentle," the man said, once again raking his eyes over Greta. "I can also be rough when it's needed," he added, letting his eyes flit to Heath. When his tongue darted out to lick his lips, Greta was glad she hadn't touched the sandwich Heath made for her.

Rosina placed a plate of cookies on the island in front of Greta and Heath. Greta shook her head. Even if she hadn't been ready to vomit, she wouldn't have wanted her thoughts impaired around this man. Rosina pursed her lips, obviously displeased, and Greta shook her head again. She couldn't care less about the witch's anger. They hadn't agreed to being anyone else's plaything.

"You'll enjoy the night much more if you have something sweet in your stomach." Though Rosina's words were soft, her gaze was hard.

"This wasn't part of the agreement, witch!" Heath spat out before Greta even realized he'd stood behind her and was making to step around her.

Without anyone moving, Heath flew backwards, toppling

over the stool he'd been sitting on and the one next to him. Greta screamed and knelt by his side. Her hands reached out to touch his chest. Thankfully, he was still breathing, though he didn't open his eyes. *Please don't be hurt.* She slid her fingers around to the back of his head to make sure he wasn't bleeding somewhere she couldn't see. "Wake up," she whispered.

Chattering behind her caught Greta's attention. She looked up to see the witch and the ogre in light conversation, both of them smiling as if they were mingling and Heath wasn't unconscious on the kitchen floor. Anger began to surge again.

"You bitch!"

Rosina turned toward her, an unbothered expression on her face. Otho whispered something in her ear, and she laughed, though her eyes never left Greta's.

"Oh, Poppet, you're absolutely delightful when you're angry. Isn't she adorable, Otho?"

Otho leaned around the island to look down at her. "She looks delicious on her knees."

Revulsion overruled any self-preservation Greta might have had, and she stood. "We agreed to stay here with you, to be at your beck and call."

"Exactly. I'm so glad that you understand better than your brother."

"Brother?" Otho licked his lips again.

"Stepbrother," Greta responded, though why she felt compelled to address his question at all, she couldn't say. Not that it mattered. Otho looked even more interested.

"Ooh, I like 'em naughty," he said, turning his attention to Rosina.

"I know, dear. That's why I've kept you away so long. I wanted them to be deliciously naughty for you."

Greta's mind reeled. What was that supposed to mean? Was she manipulating their love and mutual attraction for something even more nefarious than her own disgusting pleasure?

"I knew you'd invite me in soon enough. You don't keep your toys to yourself for very long."

"Toys are meant to be shared," Rosina said, reaching her hand down below the island before lifting her lips to his.

FIFTEEN

To be shared. The words played over and over in Greta's mind. The witch really meant to share them with that man, and who knew what his perverse interests were.

"What's going on?" Heath's voice broke through the sound of sloppy kissing happening at the end of the island. Greta jumped, startled by the fact she'd forgotten he was down there for a moment. When she turned around, Heath was sitting up, though it was easy to see he was still dazed by whatever the witch had done to throw him across the room. He rubbed the back of his head and blinked his eyes over and over as if trying to clear his mind.

"Thank goodness you're awake," Greta cried, crouching down to wrap her arms around his shoulders. As she did, she whispered in his ear. "The witch has been planning to share us with that man all along. They appear to be lovers of some sort. I don't know what to do, Heath." Though she tried to keep her voice low, her tone was shrill. Fear had taken over the anger as she worried about what the two people at the end of the island had planned.

"Oh good. He's awake. Hopefully, your little tumble has taught you a valuable lesson about watching your tone with me, Pet. Scream my name. Tell me to get on my knees when you're ready to fuck me. But don't ever think you're in charge here. My house. My rules."

Heath got to his feet and pulled Greta against him protectively. She melted into his side, letting the feel of his strength bolster her. She knew that he wasn't at his best because his body swayed a bit, but it still helped to know she wasn't alone.

"What's your plan? What do we have to do?"

The ogre grunted out a laugh and smiled. "Don't worry. I'll make sure you enjoy it."

Greta tightened her hold on Heath. She didn't believe the man for a second. There was nothing about him that said gentle or loving. Rosina may be a witch, and she may drug them into submission, but she was a mostly gentle lover. She at least gained pleasure from their pleasure. Somehow, Greta couldn't picture this man deriving pleasure from anything but pain, and she knew there were plenty of tools to inflict pain readily available in Rosina's playroom.

"Let's start all over, shall we?" Rosina gestured for them to take their seats back at the island. "Have a cookie and let's chat. I'm not so terrible as to not give you any options."

"We know all about your options," Heath muttered quietly, though the shift in Rosina's face said she'd heard him clearly.

Greta placed a hand on his leg to stop him from saying anything more that might make things worse. They were in this predicament because of Rosina's options that really left them with little choice. Better to not anger her further. They weren't in the position to argue their way out of this.

"What are our options?" Greta asked.

"Please," Rosina said, gesturing at the plate of confections. "Eat."

Greta swallowed down the nausea threatening at the very

thought of eating Rosina's tainted toffee. Then Otho grabbed one from his plate and wolfed it down like a starved dog. His eyes locked with hers as if challenging her to have one next. She wasn't convinced. It had taken a few moments for the effects to kick in the first time Rosina had given them the toffee. Since then, she'd barely given them time for it to leave their systems before plying them with more treats, leaving them in an almost constant state of arousal. Today was the first day they'd been left alone, and Greta had no desire for her mind to once again be compromised, especially not with what Rosina and Otho had planned.

Heath cleared his throat, pulling Otho's attention away, and Greta let out a ragged breath. The man unnerved her. "We're not hungry," Heath said firmly.

"Why are you so combative today, Pet?"

"You left them alone too long," Otho responded before Heath could say anything.

"Perhaps you're right, my dear. I was so overdue an outing, though. And I wanted to get us some new toys for the playroom. Besides, I'd missed you," she crooned, cupping her hand on his scarred cheek. Otho nuzzled into her touch.

"What are our options?" Greta asked again, pushing the plate a little further away from them.

Rosina chuckled. "Ah, Poppet, where is our sense of hospitality? Our guest has been left to eat alone."

"I'm sure he knew what he was doing."

"And what was that?" Otho asked, leaning his head on his hand as if bored, while he reached out and grabbed a cookie from the plate Greta had pushed away.

Greta eyed him warily, and though she wanted to chance a glance at Heath to see if he was watching, she didn't trust the man not to switch up the cookies. Otho popped the entire thing in his mouth and moaned with pleasure. He licked his lips and then his fingers before giving her what he must have thought a decadent smile. It turned her stomach at the same time she wondered whether or not the toffee had an effect on him. She couldn't imagine that Rosina had given them cookies without the aphrodisiac she'd been using all these weeks.

"Being controlled by her," Greta answered, pointing at Rosina. They both laughed, and her stomach sank.

"I could never control him. I would never control anyone. I will, however, hold people to their promises. After all, what good is a man, or woman, if his word counts for nothing?"

"Are you trying to say you haven't been drugging us since we got here?"

"Drugging you? Absolutely not! Nothing that has happened here has been against your will."

Greta scoffed at the same time she noticed Heath had been unusually silent. If anything, he should've been railing about the lies Rosina was spitting. They were lies after all. They were there, stuck in the house with a witch, because she'd drugged them, coerced them into crossing boundaries, and then giving them a painful ultimatum. None of that had happened of their own free will. She turned her face to look at Heath and found his cheeks tinged red. Was that anger or embarrassment? She reached out a hand, touching his bicep, and he flinched.

"Heath?"

He turned remorseful eyes to her. "I've wanted everything we've done. Maybe I didn't want it with someone else, and maybe we're stuck here because of the witch…"

"Watch it, Pet," Rosina interrupted, but he pushed on.

"Maybe we made some wrong choices, but she never forced me to desire you, to taste you, to fuck you, to have you for myself."

"See? I don't make anyone do anything they don't want to. I simply give options. I provide opportunities."

"Then why can't we leave?" Greta asked, imbuing each word with venom.

"Because you made an agreement. You were given a choice, and you chose to stay. I am a giving and forgiving woman and a generous lover, but I do not abide a breach of contract."

"Is it not a breach when you bring someone else in? We did not agree to additional lovers." Greta raised a brow, ready to fight the woman, magic be damned.

"Our agreement was for you to do whatever I wanted when I wanted, and you could always have each other. Today, I want you to show Otho a good time."

Greta's shoulders slumped. They'd agreed too swiftly. They hadn't thought it through. Tears stung the backs of her eyes. They were literal hostages to their own stupidity, to her libido. Next to her, Heath sighed and reached for one of the cookies. Her eyes widened, but he just shrugged. That gesture said he'd rather not be lucid for what's to come, and her heart broke for what she'd reduced him to.

"I'm sorry," she whispered and grabbed the last cookie from the plate.

'Me too,' he mouthed before swallowing the confection whole.

Sixteen

Heath

Heath hadn't wanted to eat any more of the witch's cookies. He didn't want to fall into the oblivion again, but he couldn't imagine complying with this ridiculous plan in a sober state. The way his anger continued to build, he could picture himself trying to strangle the bear of a man for even daring to touch Greta. He'd barely held back against the leering glances. Something, however, told Heath, Otho wasn't just interested in Greta. He'd caught the man eyeing him the same way, the tip of his tongue slowly working the seam of his lips. It was unnerving. Heath definitely needed something running through his system or one of them wouldn't survive the night.

"I need a shower," he said, grabbing Greta's hand and pulling her toward the door. He may have been resigned to the hell that awaited them, but he wasn't going to let her out of his sight.

Otho's body twitched, like he was about to stop their departure, but the witch put a hand on his arm. Then she turned a flirtatious smile toward them. "Don't make us wait too long."

Without another word, he led, or rather dragged, Greta from the room and toward the stairs. They needed a plan. They needed a moment to think. If only he'd had the idea before they ate the fucking cookies. There was no way he believed they weren't tainted with whatever drug the witch had been using on them. He may have had every desire they'd demonstrated these past few weeks, but he would have never acted on them had he been of sound mind. The witch was a liar, and they needed to find a way to beat her at this game, or they'd rot away here, used by whomever she decided to bring to the house.

Once they were in the bedroom, he shut the door behind him. Greta slumped on the bed, defeat written across every line of her beautiful face.

"Don't do that. Don't give up on me now." Her sad eyes met his. "C'mon, let's shower." He held out a hand for her, but she shook her head.

"You can go first." Her voice was soft, too soft.

"Together, Gretel, remember? We will find our way together." He kneeled in front of her, clasping her small hands in his. He wanted to pour all his thoughts out to her, but he had no doubt the witch had a way of listening to them. He hoped that the sound of the shower would keep her from hearing everything. When Greta finally nodded in silent acquiescence, he helped her to her feet.

Heath turned on the water, letting it run hot before they stepped inside the steam-filled enclosure. As soon as he slid the door closed, he turned to grab Greta's face. Crushing his mouth to hers, he poured out all his love and fear. He knew they didn't have much time to create a plan, but he wanted her to understand that his devotion was only to her. She was everything to him.

"They'll come looking for us soon," he said once they

separated. Greta's eyes, soft with adoration, blinked into hard bluish-green crystals. "Hopefully, she won't hear us in here if we remain quiet, but we need some kind of plan."

"I'm scared," she said while wrapping her arms around his waist. Those two words drew his anger back to the surface. How dare they scare his Greta? She'd never been scared of anything. He couldn't let that stand. He couldn't give in without a fight.

"We need a plan. I won't let him touch you."

"Did you see the way he looked at both of us? He would gladly have you too, but I think he'd be far less gentle. I couldn't stand to watch him break you. I barely survived our first night here seeing you in that cage. I'll survive anything but that."

He pulled her tightly against him. He hated the idea of letting Otho touch her as much as he was repulsed by the man himself. Still, he'd have endured anything for her.

"We still need a plan. This can't continue to go on. How many others has the witch done this to, and how many more will she do this to once we're gone?"

Greta gasped, and he guessed she'd never thought about them dying her prisoner. "Do you really think she'll never let us go?"

"Why would she?" he asked with a shrug. "She has us here captive to her whims. She uses our bodies and gets off on manipulating our love for each other. Besides, if we're here, we can't warn anyone else. There is literally no one else for miles around, no breadcrumbs to follow."

"Then how did Otho get here?"

"He's her driver." Greta looked up at him confused. "Don't you remember that she insisted on us coming home with her in her car. She had a driver. It was dark, so I didn't get a good look at him, but the guy was huge. I'm willing to bet that was Otho."

"That means, he's been around all the time. This was her

plan all along. I know I said it earlier, but it was just a feeling I got."

Heath nodded. The two of them had planned this from the beginning, and there was no way of knowing who was the one actually in charge. Did Otho have abilities too? Or was he just a man? What would he expect from them? How did he plan to use them? A shudder ran up his spine as Rosina's voice came from the other side of the bathroom door interrupting his runaway thoughts.

"We'll meet you in the playroom in five minutes, or we'll join you in the shower."

He closed his eyes and bit the inside of his cheek to keep from responding. Five minutes wasn't enough time, but they had to get some kind of plan together, else they would never be free from the witch.

"She's never going to let us go," Greta said as if the thought had just occurred to her. "We can't stay here forever."

"No, and we won't," he said, determination in his voice, though his mind had begun to spin to lustful thoughts with Greta's body pressed up against his. His cock hardened between them, and his eyes drifted low. With a low growl, he captured her lips again, unable to fight the heightened sense of arousal.

"Heath," she breathed out against his mouth before pulling away to look at him fully. Her eyes were clear, and she seemed completely unfazed by the drugs. "What are we going to do?" The question was clear, and he shook his head to chase away the haze threatening to take over.

"How?" His voice slurred. "How come you're not affected?"

"Affected by you? I am. I'm so fucking wet with wanting you, but with her banging down the door, I'm afraid to get caught on my knees again."

"No," he said, grabbing her shoulders. "Why doesn't the drug work on you?"

"It does. Just not to the extent it affects you. I've never lost myself except to my desire for you." She said the words, and he choked down a sob. She'd been lucid, at least somewhat, the entire time. She'd agreed to all of this to be with him. He didn't deserve her.

She must've felt his turmoil because she cupped his face in her hands. "I regret nothing besides waiting so long to tell you how I've felt. I wish I'd have told you sooner, so we wouldn't be stuck here."

"Our time is nearly up. We need to use your clear head to our advantage somehow."

"How about letting me decide what happens and with whom. If we find an opening for escape, we take it. If not, we just survive tonight and try again tomorrow."

He agreed knowing there was no escape while the witch lived, no escape worth seeking.

SEVENTEEN

"There you are," Rosina crooned as they stepped into the playroom. She was standing in the center of the room wearing nipple clamps and Otho was on his knees between her legs. The scene was so erotic that even with her repulsion for the people involved, Greta felt the pulse of arousal in her core. "I thought we would have to come drag you in here," the woman continued, breaking the spell that had kept Greta's eyes locked on Otho's bald head tilted up at Rosina's shaved pussy.

"Where do you want us?" Greta kept her voice even as she took a few steps into the large room. She could feel the warmth from Heath's skin as he moved in behind her, the robes that had manifested onto their bodies upon leaving the bedroom dissolving when they crossed the threshold.

"So accommodating." The witch's breathy whisper told Greta she was close to her release. "Otho here loves the taste of freshly washed pussy, and he also loves the feel of a tight ass. Which of you are willing to take his hard cock?"

So, we're just going to get straight to it, Greta thought, putting out a hand to stop Heath from stepping around her. She would be the one to take on the man as she still held out hope he would be gentler with her than with Heath. The thought withered when Otho stood, and she saw how large his cock was fully erect. She'd not taken many cocks in her ass before, other than the few times Rosina decided she needed to be doubly penetrated, but none of the dildos the witch had used even compared to him. Greta swallowed.

"You can't," Heath whispered under his breath.

"Better me than you," she responded before moving forward.

Otho's salacious grin had her wanting to run in the opposite direction, but she squared her shoulders and walked toward where he now stood crooking his finger for her to come to him. She had to think of some way to get both she and Heath out of this predicament.

"Don't look like a lamb come to slaughter, Poppet. You're made for this, and we both know how much you like to be fucked."

The witch stepped forward, and the next thing Greta knew, she was pressed up against Otho, his hands squeezing her breasts. Calloused palms rubbed over her nipples, and a soft moan left her lips. Heat crept up her neck at how quickly she'd responded to his touch. Was it the cookie? Perhaps the witch had manipulated the room or time or...there was no way she would just go from repulsed to aroused in the few seconds it took to reach where he'd stood. She started to pull back from his touch, but Rosina was suddenly at her back blocking her retreat.

"Don't think. Just feel," Rosina whispered before licking from Greta's ear down to her shoulder. At the same time Otho's lips traced upwards from her collar bone to her chin where he nipped lightly. Greta moaned again, and the grip on her breasts tightened, pinching her nipples between large fingers. At the same time, other hands traveled down from her waist to her hips and then inward to the part of her dying to be touched.

From behind her near the door, she heard Heath groan in...what was it? Frustration? Anger? Jealousy? She couldn't tell, but she knew it was killing him to watch another man touch her.

"Come watch, Pet. Or better yet, join us. We could fill all your sister's holes."

Heath growled low in his throat. It was a dangerous sound rather than a passionate one, and Greta had to stifle the shudder than ran through her body. *Please don't do something stupid*, she silently willed him. "Please," was the only thing she moaned aloud, hoping he would heed her and keep his cool. She would better be able to endure whatever they had planned if Heath was beside her, inside her.

She should've known better than to think the two people currently surrounding her, their hands on the most sensitive parts of her body, would respect their relationship or the tenuous hold Heath had on his anger. Instead, they seemed to be itching to push him beyond his restraint.

As soon as the sound of Heath's feet moving forward penetrated the haze of lust, a deep rumbly growl came from Otho, and before she could take a breath, he'd picked her up like a rag doll and carried her over to the leather bench. Her back had barely hit the hard surface when he dove face first between her legs, his tongue parting her open for him to latch onto her clit. Her back arched off the bench and "Oh. My. God." sprang from her lips.

Eighteen

Watching the ogre manhandle Greta and her scream of pleasure was like waving a red cape in front of Heath. He was ready to charge forward and tear the man apart with his bare hands. Greta moaned, and Heath's dick hardened, the anger in his veins turning to lust. Either he was going to kill someone or fuck them to death, and at this point, he couldn't care less which one happened. He stalked toward the bench where Otho had flipped Greta over to straddle it with her elbows pressed flat against the leather. The man was on his knees, his tongue buried in her ass. Heath visualized ripping out his tongue and shoving it back down the man's own throat. He'd rip his dick off and shove it up his ass. He'd...

Rosina's reproving sounds caught his attention, and he turned his head toward her. "Now is not the time for that, Pet. There will be time for your anger later when you fuck me." She was sitting on the curved bench they'd used the first time she'd manipulated him into fucking Greta. Rosina's hand was inside her panties, and he could see her rubbing small circles over her clit. The other hand was pinching and twisting first one of her nipples and then the other. Her eyes fluttered shut for a second as a wave of pleasure passed over her, and his cock twitched. He hated this woman and did not want to be turned on by her, but he couldn't help himself. Between the show she was putting on for him and the sound of Greta's pleasure, he couldn't see past the drug-induced haze. His cock was hard, and he needed to fuck something to clear his head.

Changing direction, he approached Rosina. "Suck my cock," he demanded. Surprisingly, she didn't argue or admonish him. Instead, she sat up straighter and ran the tip of her tongue between her lips.

"Fuck my mouth, Heath. Choke me with your cock and pour your anger down my throat."

He barely waited for her to finish the sentence. Taking his cock in hand, he fed it between her lips, pushing all the way into her throat. Rosina gagged slightly but didn't complain. She continued rubbing her clit and pinching her nipples as he worked himself in and out of her mouth. He listened to Greta's moans that were coming out more ragged, and his lust-filled anger grew. Heath grabbed Rosina's hair in each of his hands and held her head still. Without warning or remorse, he plowed into her mouth over and over as if he were fucking Greta's pussy. He wanted to be fucking Greta's pussy. He wanted to choke this bitch to death but not with his cock. Wrapping her hair around one of his hands, he reached the other hand down to grab her throat. He felt himself pushing into her throat and felt her gagging.

Ecstasy was written all over Rosina's face. Greta released a garbled whimper, and the corners of Rosina's mouth pulled up slightly around his cock. He didn't let up, but he looked over his shoulder while he pistoned his hips. Greta was once again on her back, and Otho had begun pushing himself inside of her tight pussy, the pussy that should belong to Heath. Greta didn't look at him or even at Otho. Her eyes were locked on the ceiling. Nothing about her body language said that she wanted what was happening, no matter how much she may have enjoyed Otho's mouth. Still, the man continued working to seat himself completely. He pulled her hips up and pushed himself in deeper, and Greta winced. A single tear slid down her cheek. Heath saw red.

Without conscious thought, his hands tightened on Rosina's hair and her throat. He squeezed while simultaneously pushing the head of his cock in until he couldn't go any further. Heath watched as Rosina's eyes flew open, her look of ecstasy replaced by one of panic. Her face turned red and splotchy. She reached her hands up and grabbed at his arms, her fingernails digging in. His eyes never left hers as the myriad of emotions passed over her face when she realized she could not get out of his grip, and the way she was seated in the hump of the bench kept her from moving to one side or the other. Her grip slackened as blood made his arms too wet to grasp, and he watched while her eyes dimmed, the life draining from her. His lips pulled back as he continued to tighten his grip. Every whimpering sound, every loud cry that came from Greta made him want to rip this bitch's head from her shoulders, but he needed Otho distracted, else they'd never get rid of them both.

When Rosina finally stopped fighting, her last bit of air gone, Heath let her mouth slide off his cock and quietly laid her out across the bench before turning around to see Otho pounding into Greta from behind. Her body was listless, and Heath's breath stalled as he wondered if the man hadn't taken Greta's life in the same way Heath had just taken Rosina's. Then Otho's voice penetrated the silence.

"Time to give your sweet cunt a break."

Nineteen

Greta took a deep breath when Otho slid his cock out of her, but she knew that whatever he planned to do next, would not bring relief. He didn't seem like the type that would care about her discomfort. He sure as fuck didn't care about her disassociation. Hell, he hadn't noticed Heath choking the life from Rosina like a cat might choke on a chicken bone. He didn't see her face turn red or her fingernails draw blood from Heath's arms. Otho didn't seem to notice Rosina's garbled cries for help as her airway was cut off, he simply flipped Greta from her stomach to her back again, so he could squeeze her tits. He didn't notice any of it, but Greta did.

She noticed, and she whimpered a little louder. She let her moans come more frequently, as she watched Heath end the woman who had kidnapped and tormented them for weeks. Greta might have been dismayed by his murderous confessions earlier, but she reveled in the sight of the veins popping out on his forearms as he held Rosina in place. She might not have wanted to admit it, but even she knew the only way to get out of this house now was to kill the witch.

Now, they simply had to dispatch with this ogre of a man. Heath moved in her periphery, but she didn't want to draw attention to him. Otho was too strong for there to be a fair fight between them.

Greta gasped when Otho grabbed her hips once again. She could feel his momentum preparing to flip her over, and fear had her throat closing up. The witch's warning of his proclivity for anal making her stiffen her entire body to try and keep him from moving her. He looked down at her with a gleam in his eye.

"Ooh, I like a little fight with my play. I was afraid Rosina had taken all the fight out of you both. She does that far too often."

He said the words and started to turn his head to look back toward where the witch's limp body molded into the bench's curves at odd angles. Greta began wiggling as if trying to get out of his grasp, hoping to pull his attention back to her. He smiled, baring his teeth like a cat proudly toying with its prey. His grip tightened, and he flipped her halfway over. A sharp slap resounded through the room as his huge hand connected to her ass cheek making her whole body vibrate. She cried out, the shock making her pliable in his hands once again. He flipped her the rest of the way over and slapped the other cheek just as hard. Her eyes burned from unshed tears, and she had to fight to keep them open.

"Keep fighting. It will make me enjoy your punishment even more. I'm going to wreck that tight asshole of yours and watch those plump cheeks jiggle the whole time."

The dam holding back the tears broke, and they now streamed down her face. She had no time to wonder where Heath was when Otho spit on her ass, and she felt his saliva run down between her cheeks. No, no, no, this couldn't be happening. He couldn't be planning to fuck her ass with only his saliva as lube. He'd literally split her open. Then, his hands were rubbing her ass, massaging his spit into her puckered hole as he slid a finger in trying to push past the tight ring. Every muscle in her body screamed for her to tense up, to fight him off, but she knew that would only make it worse.

"So tight around my finger. You're going to choke my cock deliciously."

His words had bile rising into her throat, and she almost wished Rosina were still alive. The witch enjoyed toying with them too much to let any real damage be done. But it was too late for that. And where was Heath? Just then, Otho froze above her, and she heard him sniff in deeply.

"Dammit, Rosina, did you leave cookies in the oven again?" his deep voice bellowed, followed by a higher pitched, "What the fuck?" before he ripped his finger from Greta's ass.

Greta opened her eyes from where she had been squeezing them shut against the sting of Otho's unwanted and unprepped assault. The fear of what was to come next had her frozen until she caught movement in her periphery again. This time it came from the other side away from where the witch lay. Heath moved quickly behind Otho where she could no longer see him. She lifted her head from the bench, willing her limbs to move as well when Otho stepped from behind her. The smell of smoke assaulted her nostrils. Something was happening, and she couldn't just lay there.

"Move Greta. Get your ass up and move," she told herself, whispering to keep from drawing Otho's attention back to her.

"Rosina?" Otho's voice had taken on a concerned tone and then one of anger when he called her name again.

The room shook as he dropped to his knees next to the witch's lifeless body, and Greta held her breath. As slowly as possible, she lifted her torso from the bench with wobbly arms and began to slide her left leg across the leather. She feared the sound of her skin squeaking on the material. It didn't matter though, Otho hadn't forgotten about her.

"Looks like he left you to face his punishment," the ogre said, turning his face to lock eyes with her. There had been a slight hint of sadness in his gaze before it hardened. "I will fuck the life out of you and leave your corpse on his doorstep."

His body turned slightly to face her, but before he could once again climb to his feet, Heath reached around the man's neck. "The only corpse being left is yours," Heath ground out as his hand slid across Otho's throat. The giant of a man opened his mouth, but he choked instead. Blood gushed from the thin line Heath had made that was now gaping open. Greta had expected to see fear on the man's face, but his was the look of resignation. He started to topple forward, but he steadied himself by grabbing onto Rosina's thigh before turning to lay his body out across hers. Blood pooled around him and covered Rosina in a blanket of red the same way her fiery locks were splayed out across the bench.

Greta's eyes stayed pinned on their captors until Heath slid behind her, wrapping his arms around her torso. Heath said something to her, but she couldn't understand him. He pulled her naked body against his, lifting her from where she was frozen half on and half off the bench. He said something else, and there seemed to be an urgency to his tone. Though she could hear his voice, the words were garbled, like she was underwater. His hand clasped her cheek, forcing her to look at him. Still, she couldn't make sense of his words. She lifted her hand to point toward Rosina and Otho, but when she tried to turn her head, he held her steady, laying his forehead against hers. It was like time stood still for them. At least until a loud crash broke through her consciousness.

Suddenly, she was once again there, in the moment with all the pain and sound whooshing back into her brain. Her body ached, her extremities were heavy, and her head hurt.

She focused her gaze on Heath who held her cradled in his arms, worry etched on his face. He smiled down at her, but it was tight. Then he looked over his shoulder.

"What's wrong?" She managed to eke out through dry lips.

"Baby, we gotta go. We have to go now."

The urgency in his voice had concern creeping up her spine, but she tamped it down. Putting her hand to his cheek, she lifted her face to lightly kiss his lips. "We're safe, Heath. We're free. You..."

"No, we're not safe. We have to get out of this house."

He looked over his shoulder again as another loud popping sound came from down the hall.

"What was that?" She cried.

He stood, pulling her to her feet. "Can you walk?"

She tested her legs. They were still a bit wobbly, but she was able to hold up her own weight. Trying to ignore the visions of how she'd become so unsteady, she forced herself to focus on Heath's face. "Yes, I think so."

Heath said nothing, simply took her hand and led her through the doorway. As soon as they crossed the threshold robes covered their bodies and slippers adorned their feet. Greta gasped at the sudden sensation against her skin as she had every time the house clothed them, but Heath urged her forward. They were just two steps from the hallway that led to the front door when the door to the kitchen sizzled, and flames licked around it.

"Oh my god! The house is on fire!"

"That's what I was trying to tell you. We have to go!"

One more step, and the door sucked inward, heat barreling into them as flames engulfed the doorframe. "Shit!" they both exclaimed. There was no way for them to get past the kitchen to the hallway that led to the front door. That entire portion of the house was on fire. There was also no escape back the way they came. Greta pulled open the only other door on the hall. A set of stairs led down into a dark abyss, and she shuddered, ready to close the door, but then a cool breeze wafted past them. They might find themselves stuck down there, but it had to be safer than staying up here while the house burned down around them.

"Down here," she choked out while pulling on Heath's hand.

Smoke had begun to completely fill the space now that the kitchen door was open and no longer containing anything. Heath looked down the stairs and then back at her, fear etched in the lines between his brows.

"Are you sure?"

"Do you have a better idea?"

She didn't wait for him to respond, just took the first tentative step. The stair felt sturdy enough, so she took another one, giving Heath a chance to follow her down. They had to get below the smoke. Her hand felt along the wall trying to find a light switch, but there wasn't one.

"We have to close the door to keep the smoke from filling the basement," she said. Her voice was gravely, and her chest was heavy. The only sign that Heath even heard her was the door slamming above.

"I'm not sure it'll hold for long," he said quietly between coughs.

Greta paused and released his hand for a moment. She had no idea how much further they'd have to descend to find the basement floor, but she quickly pulled off the robe and passed it to Heath. "Put this under the door." It wouldn't do much, but it might buy them a few minutes. Moments later, Heath took in a deep, raspy breath and fell into a coughing fit. He reached out and grabbed her shoulders.

They had to get off these stairs before they teetered to their deaths.

The first ten slow steps down, with Heath's weight on her shoulders, seemed to take an hour. Wood above their head splintered and they could hear walls caving in. The fire hadn't yet consumed the basement door, but it was only a matter of time. They had to keep moving. Five more steps, and light from the fire above created an aura around them. Still, she couldn't see the floor. *Dammit, how much further did they have to go?*

She stopped short, and Heath nearly toppled her over when her foot connected evenly with solid ground. Stepping out of the way, so Heath could join her on the floor, she took in the view above them. Angry, red light streamed in around the door, and rivulets of smoke seeped through the cracks, but they didn't seem to be expanding into the basement like they had from the kitchen into the hall. It was like something was holding them back. Once again, a cool breeze passed across her face. Where was it coming from?

Heath must have felt it at the same time because he gritted out, "There must be a window or door down here."

She wanted to give him a snarky retort about him stating the obvious, but his next round of coughs held her tongue. It was far more important they find a way out. Grabbing Heath's hand again, she shuffled forward, her other arm outstretched, almost flailing around until she walked into a table in the middle of the floor. She had no idea how much time had passed, but it felt like they were walking in circles and getting nowhere. Surely, there had to be another exit along the walls. How had they not found it yet?

"There's that breeze again," Heath said from her side. "It came from this direction."

He began pulling her to the right, and she wanted to scream that they had already been down every shadowed aisle, every dark crevice, and along every stone wall.

Somehow, the fire hadn't made its way through into the basement, nor could they hear it anymore. Maybe if they waited long enough, they could just make their way back up the stairs. It would have to burn out eventually, right?

"Here. There's a door here."

Heath yanked her to stand next to him, stretching out her arm until she brushed against something metal rather than cinderblock. She pulled her hand free from his grip and felt around, recognizing the outline of an outside cellar door. Had they finally found their escape route?

"Here's the handle!" she cried, grabbing it with both hands and pulling with all her might. It didn't move. "It's stuck."

Heath reached for her in the dark and touched his way to where her hands held the metal rod. Though their eyes had adjusted to recognize deeper shadows in the dark, they still couldn't see anything clearly. She could, however, catch the movement of his hands as he felt around the base of the rod.

"Don't pull, twist." He matched his words to action by wrapping his hands around hers and initiating the twisting movement. She still heard the rattle in his chest as he coughed at the exertion, but he seemed too focused to notice. Finally, the lever moved, and the door creaked as if it hadn't been opened in ages. "Push," Heath instructed, and she did. More cool air entered the space. One more shove, and the doors flew open, giving them a beautiful view of the clear night sky that they hadn't seen in weeks.

TWENTY

Goosebumps spread across Greta's skin. The bathwater had gone from scalding to arctic, and yet she couldn't stop reliving the nightmare. Daymare? Constant-mare? It wasn't like she could ever escape it, and she wasn't the only one. She regularly found Heath staring off into space or woke to him running in his sleep. He never wanted to talk about it, so she, too, was stuck inside her own head reliving it all silently.

They'd rejoiced when they climbed out of the cellar into the crisp night air. The excitement didn't last for long, though. Yes, they'd escaped the house and were safe from the fire, but they weren't out of the woods. Heath's coughs had kept them from getting too far. He'd had to stop fifty yards away and sit in the grass. Thankfully, they weren't naked, which seemed a crazy thing to be thankful for, but it was the first thing Heath had said since they'd stepped out onto the gravel that encircled the house.

Heath laughed and pulled on the fabric of her dress. "Nice of the house to give us back our clothes from the night we came here."

She responded with a chuckle she didn't feel. She wanted to burn the dress, to pull it off and throw it into the flames less than a football field away from them with the hope the memories of that night and the subsequent weeks would burn away as well. Instead, she burrowed into his side as they sat there silently watching the house collapse in on itself.

Hours, or maybe minutes, later, smoke trickled from the destroyed cottage. Though the smell clung to them, the air was clear enough for them to take in deep breaths, and Heath's breathing was coming easier. Still, they sat there, eyes fixed on the smoldering house.

"What happens now?" she asked.

"We have to find our way out of here and make it home," Heath responded as if her question were as simple as asking what was for dinner.

She turned to look at him. "You know that's not what I mean."

He took a shuddering breath and gave her a sad smile. "I know, but I don't have an answer, at least not a good one."

Greta understood his noncommittal response. The witch was dead, but that didn't mean their contract was null since they'd been the ones to break it, well, Heath had. Getting out of the house meant that their clothes returned to them as if nothing happened, but she sure didn't feel like the same woman who'd arrived here that night. What was the likelihood they'd return to find their lives exactly as they left them?

She sighed. "What do you want to happen, Heath?"

At first, he didn't move. When he didn't respond for several seconds, she turned herself completely to make sure he was still breathing. His eyes just stared forward for an uncomfortable amount of time before he gave her an answer.

"I want what I've always wanted. You. But I won't lie and say I'm not afraid I won't get to have that." She straddled his lap, grateful that the dress was short enough to not constrict her movements, and wrapped her arms around his neck. He held her back and sobbed. "I don't deserve you. I'm not safe. My anger..." he trailed off.

"Your anger is what saved us. You have always protected me.

You've always been my safe place. You will always be home for me, Heath."

"How? How are you not scared of me? I'm scared of me."

"You will never hurt me, of that I have no doubt. Rosina tried. She drugged you, drove you to a frenzy, and yet you still never hurt me. Instead, it was me who put you in that position. If either of us is unsafe for the other, it's me."

He pulled her closer, burying his face in her chest and shaking his head. Greta kissed his temple before pulling his face up, so they were eye to eye. "I don't know what's going to happen when we leave these grounds. I don't know if her spell, our contract, hell, any of it will follow us home." She took a shuddering breath. "I do know that I love you. I've always loved you, and I don't want to forget how you feel inside me." A single tear slipped from the corner of her eye, and Heath wiped it away. She placed her lips against his and held them there for several moments before pulling away.

He gave her a sad smile. "I hate that all my memories of us, of you writhing beneath me will be tainted by her presence. I wish there was a spell to forget it all, but not you, never you." The last part came out as a choked sob.

"Then give me a memory that's just us before we go home to find out this nightmare is neverending."

Before she could get all the words out, Heath's mouth was on hers, and it wasn't the soft touching of lips she'd given him earlier. His mouth was hot, his tongue penetrating her parted lips in a frenzy that she responded to eagerly. He pulled down the top of her dress and squeezed her breasts, pinching her nipples into taut peaks. She moaned, her core contracting at every tweak, and when he pulled one of the nubs into his mouth, she cried out his name.

Without leaving his lap, she reached down between them and undid his jeans. It wasn't easy with him sitting up holding her, but she managed. When she couldn't pull his cock out, though, she pushed him to the ground, so she could wriggle his waistband down over his ass. He didn't complain about being bare-assed on the ground, or at least, he didn't get a chance to because she lifted *herself enough to notch him at her entrance and settle herself onto him. It took some wiggling and rocking of their hips to get him fully seated inside of her, but as soon as he was, they both sighed.*

"You're so fucking perfect," he said, love and adoration pouring from him.

She soaked up his praise and began moving her hips back and forth. It wouldn't be long before she came, and by the way he was panting beneath her, he wasn't going to last either. Still, she reveled in the feel of him, the sounds he was making, and the way his hands dug into her flesh. They were here together, free from the witch, and he was hers completely. If she was going to suffer nightmares from everything that happened to them the past few weeks, let her also have this dream to hold onto.

And she did remember that moment. She remembered it every time she reached for Heath, and he was gone, whether it was to work or downstairs. She remembered it when she couldn't have him immediately. His moans plagued her in the shower and each time she went grocery shopping, but when he was beside her, only the nightmares appeared.

They may have escaped the witch's grasp, but they didn't escape her promise.

Choose Your Own Ending

As a romance author, I know the expected conventions that make us love Romance as a genre, not just as an element. As a long-time lover of fairytales, I also know they are not always happy at the end. In true fairytales, the hero doesn't always win, and the princess isn't always whole at the end. There are things that make us question our beliefs and dreams that morph into nightmares. Both can be true, and yet, we sometimes get a choice of which ending we choose to accept.

Thus, I have written two separate endings for this story: (1) A fairytale ending, full of suspense that leaves you questioning what you think you know, and (2) an optimistic ending that makes you believe Heath and Greta can have their happily ever after regardless of all the obstacles they had to overcome. You can read both or choose your own path. If you want the original fairytale ending, turn the page and read Heath's Fairytale Ending. If you need that spark of hope, skip to the Happily Ever After Ending. Either way, I hope you find what you're looking for at the end of this tale.

Fairytale Ending

Heath walked in the door to the smell of fresh-baked cookies. He smiled, but sadness clutched at his chest. Greta must have had a good day because she hadn't baked anything for weeks. In fact, she hadn't wanted to touch any baked goods since they'd escaped the witch's gingerbread-looking house. He'd had to push her to dig her fingers into the soft dough, and he held her while she wept and kneaded. Before that fateful night, she'd been considering starting her own online bakery. Now, six months later, she'd finally baked something without his coaxing. The thought pushed away the sadness. He put the vase he'd been carrying down on the table alongside his keys and locked the door behind him.

Music blared from the top of the stairs, and he could hear Greta shuffling around up there. He had no doubt that she was dancing around in nothing but a towel, her damp hair clinging to her shoulders, and his cock stiffened. He'd told her to be ready for a night out, but he spent the entire day expecting for her to argue against it. She hadn't been out of the apartment since their escape. She swore that someone was watching them from the moment they'd escaped the witch's property, but there was no way he wasn't going to take her out for her birthday. He would not let that crazy time ruin the rest of their lives.

He stepped into the kitchen and found a stack of boxes on the counter next to a tray of freshly baked cookies. There was a picture of a gingerbread house with the name Breadcrumbs stamped across the top of the boxes. He chuckled to himself and popped one of the cookies in his mouth before making his way upstairs. He found her standing in front of the full-length mirror in nothing but a bra and panties, all her suppleness on display, much like she had been the very first time he'd kissed her skin. His mouth went dry, and his cock hardened at the sight. Greta was still the most beautiful woman he'd ever seen, and it didn't matter how many years passed, he knew she'd always take his breath away.

The dress she had laid out on the bed made him clench his teeth. "Who are you trying to impress, Gretel?"

Rather than the surprised response he expected, Greta looked up at him through the mirror and smirked, her pupils dilating. "You."

Heath pushed off the door jamb and sauntered toward her. With each step, her chest rose and fell. When he pressed his body against hers, her breath hitched, and she pulled her lip between her teeth. Tilting his head to the side, he placed his lips where her neck and shoulder meet before trailing soft kisses up toward her ear.

"Heath."

The word came out breathy, and his cock twitched in response. He wrapped his arms around her and pressed his hand against her lower stomach, so her ass pushed back against him. A soft moan escaped her lips, and he smiled against her neck before bringing his mouth to her ear.

"Does that feel like you need to impress me, Gretel? You

couldn't get rid of me if you tried." He kissed his way back down her neck and out onto her shoulder before turning her around to face him. With both of his hands now on her ass, he walked her back toward the bed. "I will always find my way back to you." He kissed her lips. "It's like that first taste of your skin all those years ago left a trail of breadcrumbs for me to follow until I could have my fill." When her calves hit the bed, he pressed her down onto it and began kissing his way down her body. Her hands fisted in his hair, guiding him toward the prize he was already planning to claim, the one that belonged to him.

When his face reached the apex of her thighs, he held his nose against her panties and inhaled deeply. She whimpered in that way he hadn't heard for months outside of his daydreams. Tonight, however, he was determined to hear it over and over again. He pushed her thighs open with his hands and placed open mouth kisses in the creases on either side of her pussy. "You smell better than all the baking you did today," he said before sliding her panties to the side, opening her plump lips to him. His mouth watered. "And you taste better than those cookies you left on the counter."

Greta cried out in surprise, but he didn't register her response. He buried his face in her pussy, lapping up her arousal before latching onto her clit. She wriggled beneath him, and he growled, turned on by her scent and her taste. The need for her was the only thing he could feel. She said his name over and over, and he reveled in it. She was his completely, and he was going to devour her. He slid two fingers inside of her and began pumping them in and out, searching for the ridge that would have her screaming.

"You taste so fucking good. I want to drink every drop of you."

"Heath. Baby. Please. Lis..."

She didn't get to finish the words as he once again latched onto her clit, his fingers working in and out. He didn't want her speaking. He wanted her screaming his name. He wanted her coming on his cock.

"Cookies...not..."

What the fuck was she talking about? She shouldn't be talking about cookies. She should be squeezing his fingers and squirting all over his tongue.

"Heath. Please. Stop."

What? No. That couldn't be right. Greta would never tell him to stop. She loved him. She loved this. She was his.

Greta's hands were again in his hair, but rather than pulling him against her, she was trying to push him away. The pain from his scalp combined with her repeated call for him to stop wormed their way into his brain until he looked up at her face. Tears trailed down her cheeks, and her mascara ran along with them. He stared at her and watched her lip quiver for what felt like forever until his brain fully registered that something was wrong. He lifted his mouth from her pussy and pulled out his fingers.

"Baby, what's...what's going on? Did I hurt you?"

Soft sobs escaped from her lips. No. No. No. He couldn't have hurt her. He wouldn't hurt her. He climbed up her body until he was eye level with her, and though his cock strained between them, ready to be buried inside her, Heath forced himself to focus on her face.

"Greta, baby. What's wrong?"

She stared at him, eyes wide with fear. Was she afraid of him? Fuck! What had he done?

"Talk to me, Greta. Please."

She took a few deep breaths before responding in a whisper so quiet, he almost didn't hear her.

"I didn't make the cookies."

HEA Ending

Heath

Heath walked in the door to the smell of fresh-baked cookies. He smiled, but sadness clutched at his chest. Greta hadn't baked anything in what seemed like forever. In fact, she hadn't wanted to touch any baked goods since they'd escaped the witch's gingerbread-looking house. He'd had to force her to dig her fingers into some soft dough weeks ago, and then he'd held her while she wept and kneaded. Before that fateful night when they'd gone to the club and met Rosina, Greta had been considering starting her own online bakery. Now, six months later, she'd finally baked something without his coaxing. The thought pushed away the sadness. He put the vase he'd been carrying down on the table alongside his keys and locked the door behind him.

Music blared from the top of the stairs, and he could hear Greta shuffling around up there. He had no doubt that she was dancing around in nothing but a towel, her damp hair clinging to her shoulders the same way it always has, and his cock stiffened at the image. He'd told her to be ready for a night out, but he spent the entire day expecting her to argue against it. She hadn't been out of the apartment since their escape, but there was no way he wasn't going to take her out for her birthday. He would not let the nightmare ruin the rest of their lives.

When he stepped into the kitchen, he found a stack of boxes on the counter next to a tray of freshly baked cookies. There was a picture of a gingerbread house with the name Breadcrumbs stamped across the top of the boxes. He chuckled to himself and popped one of the cookies in his mouth before making his way upstairs with two more in his hand.

He found her standing in front of the full-length mirror in nothing but a bra and panties, all of her suppleness on display, much like she had been the very first time he'd kissed her skin. His mouth went dry, and his cock grew painfully hard at the sight. Greta was still the most beautiful woman he'd ever seen, and it didn't matter how many years passed, he knew she'd always take his breath away.

He looked at the dress she had laid out on the bed and growled. "Who are you trying to impress, Gretel?"

Rather than the surprised response he expected, Greta looked up at him through the mirror and smirked, her pupils dilating. "You."

Heath pushed off the door jamb and sauntered toward her, popping the last cookie in his mouth. With each step, her chest rose and fell. When he pressed his body against hers, her breath hitched, and she pulled her lip between her teeth. Tilting his head to the side, he placed his lips where her neck and shoulder meet before trailing soft kisses up toward her ear.

"Heath."

The word came out breathy, and his cock twitched in response. It had been so long since he'd touched her, since their bodies had responded to each other. They'd spent the first weeks back home trying to force the physical intimacy their brains so desperately wanted, but it became a painful reminder of their time with Rosina rather than a beautiful reflection of their love for each other. Right now, though, all he could think about was burying himself inside of her, of licking her clean. He wrapped his arms around her and pressed his hand against her lower stomach, so her ass pushed back against him. A soft moan escaped her lips, and he smiled against her neck before bringing his mouth to her ear.

"Does that feel like you need to impress me, Gretel? You couldn't get rid of me if you tried." He kissed his way back down her neck and out onto her shoulder before turning her around to face him. With both his hands now on her ass, he walked her back toward the bed. "I will always find my way back to you." He kissed her lips.

"You taste like cookies," she said quietly when he'd released her mouth and began trailing kisses down her neck again.

"Give me a few seconds, and I'm going to taste like your cookie." He hummed in satisfaction when she gasped. It had been far too long since he'd heard that sound, far too long since he'd tasted her. "It's like that first taste of your skin all those years ago left a trail of breadcrumbs for me to follow until I could have my fill. I will never get enough."

Her calves hit the bed, and he pressed her down onto it. He began kissing his way down her body, pulling her breasts out to suck on her peaked nipples. Her hands fisted in his hair, guiding him toward the prize he had already planned to claim, the one that belonged to him. Rather than lowering his body further, though, he guided her up the bed.

When his face reached the apex of her thighs, he held his nose against her panties and inhaled deeply. She whimpered in that way he hadn't heard outside of his daydreams. Tonight, however, he was determined to hear it over and over again. He pushed her thighs open with his hands and placed open-mouth kisses in the creases on either side of her pussy. "You smell better than all the baking you did today," he said before sliding her panties to the side, opening her plump lips to him. His mouth watered. "And you taste better than those cookies you left on the counter."

Greta cried out in surprise and said something about the cookies working, but he didn't register her words. He buried his face in her pussy, lapping up her arousal before latching onto her clit. She wriggled beneath him, and he growled, turned on by her scent and her taste. The need for her was the only thing he could feel. She said his name over and over, and he reveled in it. She was his completely, and he was going to devour her. He slid two fingers inside of her and began pumping them in and out, searching for the ridge that would have her screaming.

"You taste so fucking good. I want to drink every drop of you."

"Yes. Please don't…"

She didn't finish the sentence, as he once again latched onto her clit, his fingers working in and out. He didn't want her speaking. He wanted her screaming his name. He wanted her coming on his cock.

"Heath…fuck!"

He growled around her clit, the animalistic need to possess her driving him on. He felt her tense, her walls tightening around his fingers. 'Please' became a chant on her lips, and when the pulsations started, he slid his tongue to her entrance, letting her come in his mouth.

"Heath, I need you."

Finally, the words he'd been dying to hear. The ones his mind conjured to torment him daily. He knew she loved him, knew she was his, but he'd needed her to want him.

Greta's hands were again in his hair, trying to pull him back up her body. The pain from his scalp wormed its way into his brain until he finally looked up at her face. The need in her eyes was mesmerizing, and his dick screamed to give her what she needed. He lifted his mouth from her pussy and pulled out his fingers.

"Baby?" His voice was gravely, and he could see the effect that one word had on her as she squirmed beneath him. Her hands had released his hair and were now pulling at his head and then his shoulders as he crawled up her body, slowly stalking her mouth. "Do you want this cock, Gretel? Have you been lost without it?"

A whimper escaped her lips, and satisfaction tickled his spine when she whispered 'yes.' Rather than stopping when his mouth was high enough to claim hers, he continued climbing over her until he was seated above her chest. His cock throbbed as it sat bobbing above her lips.

"Show me how badly you've needed this cock."

She stared at him, eyes hooded with desire. She didn't even blink, just grabbed his hard shaft and gave it a tug. He leaned forward, and when her tongue traced the line between his balls, he nearly collapsed forward. Then she wrapped her lips around his sack, and he had to grip the headboard.

"Fuck, Greta. Holy fuck!"

She let out a satisfied moan that sent shivers through his entire body. He was going to come, and she hadn't even touched his cock with her lips yet. Just when he thought he couldn't hold himself back anymore, she released his balls and tilted her head up. He looked down to see her smirking up at him.

"Did you like that, Hansel?"

The chuckle threatening to leave his mouth at her ludicrous question and snarky response to him calling her Gretel stuck in his throat when she grabbed his shaft and gave it a few pumps before pressing the head of his cock to her lips. She flicked her tongue along the slit, lapping up the bead of precum her ball sucking had produced.

"Mmmm," she moaned. "You're not the only one who's

been looking for a way back." Her lips trailed kisses from the tip of his cock to the base. "I'd been searching for breadcrumbs for weeks, but nothing worked."

She let her tongue trail up in the opposite direction, and he couldn't hold back a groan. She was once again working him up, his balls tightening, only for her to leave him panting to say something more.

"Greta. Baby. Shit." He dragged out the words, straining against his own need. "I'm not gonna last if you keep doing that."

"I realized that I wasn't supposed to be looking for the breadcrumbs. It was my job to leave them for you to find, something to remind your senses what your brain has always known."

Her hands worked up and down his shaft, caressing his swollen bulb and then squeezing each time they touched bottom. He moaned but never broke eye contact.

"What was it my brain has always known, Greta?"

She licked her lips. "That I have always belonged to you. That every part of me aches for you the same way you've always ached for me. That staying away from each other was like locking ourselves in cages."

She paused for a moment and pulled her lip between her teeth. The sheen of unshed tears had him wanting to climb off and wrap her in his arms, but she hadn't released his cock. She continued stroking it at the most tantalizingly slow pace.

"Every nightmare I have is about losing you. Every moment spent not touching you was like subsisting on stale bread. Then I realized that what we have, what we are together is sweet. Cookies are what brought you to me the first time, so I took a chance."

A shuddering breath escaped his lungs as he opened his mouth to tell her how much he loved her, but she stopped him by popping his cock into her mouth and swirling her tongue around the rim of his head. The entire world stopped while he watched the only woman he'd ever loved suck him off like her life depended on it.

"Fuuuck," was all he could say, and when she reached around to grab his ass and pull him in until he touched the back of her throat, he had no more words. He ceased to think, to breathe, to exist. All he could do was feel.

His hips began moving of their own accord, and Greta moaned, humming in satisfaction. Shivers ran up his spine, and his balls pulled up tight. He wanted to warn her, to give her a chance to release his cock, but all that came out was her name as he coated her throat with his cum. He couldn't even scream. He simply stared down at her in awe, his whole body convulsing with the power of his release. She sucked down every drop.

When he was finally spent, his cock no longer throbbing, she pulled him from her mouth with a dramatic pop and smiled up at him with a raised brow. For several seconds, they stared at each other, and just when the corners of her mouth began to drop, he burst out laughing. She joined him, and he rolled off her, allowing himself to slump down at her side.

GRETA

Greta snuggled into him.

"Thank you," he said once his heart rate had stabilized, and his breathing had relaxed.

"For what, the best orgasm of your life?" she asked, laughter in her tone.

"No," he said, tickling her sides like he had when they were younger. "Thank you for showing me the way home. I said I'd always find you, but I didn't realize I was also lost."

She gave him a small smile and shrugged. "What can I say? I'd waited too long to be fully loved by you to give it up that easily."

He kissed her nose. "I love you so much. I'm sorry it took so long to show it."

"If I had known cookies were the key to getting you in my bed, I'd have opened a bakery years ago."

"If I had known how good your cookie tasted, I'd have chained myself to your bed."

"Oh really?"

Greta's head tilted to the side, and there was a wicked gleam in her eye. She pushed him onto his back. His hands came up to her sides, but she guided them up toward the wrought iron headboard he'd used to stabilize himself earlier.

"Grab the headboard and don't let go, unless you want to be chained to my bed for real."

He wasted no time wrapping his fingers around the twisted bars, and she watched his cock get hard at the threat. "What're you going to do to me?"

"I'm going to make up for lost time."

She positioned herself so her pussy lips kissed along his shaft, and she watched his face. Fascination and desire mixed with curiosity in his eyes, and his brows furrowed. She pursed her lips and began working her hips back and forth, enjoying the friction of his length along her slit. He let out a small moan, but it was tinged with something else. When he opened his mouth, and she saw the question in his gaze, she put her finger over his lips.

"We will work it all out together. For now, stop thinking and just feel." With those words, she lifted herself to notch him at her entrance and settled down onto him. They both sighed with contentment before rocking themselves into oblivion.

And they lived happily ever after.

Acknowledgments

I always have to acknowledge the rest of Roberts Row (Gracie Cooper, Britton Brinkley, and Ashley Willow) for always encouraging me to push things just a little bit further. I won't say I blame them for half the stuff that comes out under this name. I will simply say I acknowledge their involvement and contributions to my delusions.

Speaking of acknowledging delusional encouragement…I have to give a shout out to Vanessa and Destiny. Not only do they listen to us prattle on about random characters and plot points every night, but they keep asking for more. If you've ever been on one of our TikTok lives, you've probably chatted with them down in the comments. They both were early readers of this book, as well as Gracie, and I couldn't be more grateful for the feedback and love.

There are also a couple other authors who regularly spend time with us, and were there for most of the conjuring of this story. These are Friends of The Row who also deserve some love: Roberta Timmons, Tink Mauveen, and Willow Asteria.

Last but never least, is the man who lets me do my thing and never complains when I fall into bed at 2am after typing my heart out. He listens to my frustrations and asks, "so what can you do differently to make it better next time." Usually that's all it takes to get me back on track. Thanks, Babe!

Other Titles by the Author

Currently Available

Carol's Christmas Awakening
Clarissa and the Wallflower
Love with a Vengeance
You've Got Bookmail
Shar's Story

Coming Soon

Fall 2025: A 2nd Tempting Tale (yet untitled)
October 13, 2025: Josefina, a spooky tale of a motorcycle coven with
shadow magic

Coming Spring 2026
Expanded Rereleases of all 4 Cole County novellas. If you thought you
loved Leya's stories in the anthologies, you will love them more in their
full form with their own titles. Watch for the series Cole County Memories
to be quick released in 2026.

About the Author

Follow Leya all over social media:
https://linktr.ee/LeyaLayneAuthor

Leya Layne's love of a Happily Ever After started with Disney. Then she found romance novels in her early teens thanks to a bag of Harlequin novels hidden under her grandmother's dresser. She got her HEA fix for the rest of her teen years thanks to a well-worn library card.

Though she is currently publishing contemporary romances that have been described as Hot Hallmark, don't be surprised to see her delve into historical or paranormal in the future. The possibilities are endless, but the one thing she'll promise is that they'll all be spicy!

www.ingramcontent.com/pod-product-compliance
Lightning Source LLC
Chambersburg PA
CBHW031056310726

48969CB00007B/2296